The Bloody Man

Bevan Amberhill

A sergeant
(Alan Wales)

The Bloody Man

A Jean-Claude Keyes Mystery

by Bevan Amberhill

A MIDNIGHT ORIGINAL MYSTERY
The Mercury Press

§

The Bloody Man is a work of fiction. All characters are products of the author's imagination. Any resemblance between these characters and actual persons, living or dead, is purely coincidental.

The City of Stratford, Ontario, and its world-renowned Shakespearean Festival are real places. The author has taken small liberties with geography, for the purposes of the story.

The author wishes to acknowledge the assistance of the Ontario Arts Council during the writing of this book.
§

The publisher gratefully acknowledges the financial assistance of the Canada Council, the Ontario Arts Council, and the Government of Ontario through the Ontario Publishing Centre.

Edited by Beverley Daurio
Frontispiece by Virgil Burnett
Cover design by Ted Glaszewski

Typeset in Goudy Old Style by TASK
Printed and bound in Canada by Metropole Litho
Printed on acid-free paper

Second Printing, August, 1994
2 3 4 5 97 96 95 94

Canadian Cataloguing in Publication Data:
Amberhill, Bevan
The bloody man
ISBN 1-55128-007-8
I. Title.
PS8551.M24B5 1993 C813'.54 C93-094761-4
PR9199.3.A53B5 1993

Represented in Canada by the Literary Press Group

Distributed in Canada by General Publishing
and in the United States by Inland Book Company (selected titles)

The Mercury Press
137 Birmingham Street
Stratford, Ontario
Canada N5A 2T1

The Bloody Man

DRAMATIS PERSONAE

JEAN-CLAUDE KEYES . . Former actor, now writer

SEAMUS O'REILLY . . . . Grand old actor

JULIA . . . . Waitress

BRUNO . . . . Bartender

ALAN WALES . . . . . . Actor

BETTY BEARDSLEY . . . Owner BB's Bed & Breakfast

ALESSANDRA EDEL . . . Actress

HOBART PORLISS . . . . Director

GEORGE BROCKEN . . . Designer

GRACE LOCKHARDT . . Dresser

KIRI (JANIE) ELLISON . . Stripper

FRANKIE & JO . . . . . . Shopkeepers

Actors, Actresses, Shopkeepers, Party-goers, Swans, &c.

PROLOGUE
Toronto, Union Station

Union Station's ever-shifting population surged and buzzed around Jean-Claude Keyes as he sat across from Gate Six, waiting for the train to Stratford.

On his lap was a stack of 8½ X 11" paper, and a glossy brochure. The stack was the manuscript of his work-in-progress, the pamphlet a guide to this season's Stratford Shakespearean Festival, a season drawing rapidly to a close. Claude made a final mark in red ink on the manuscript, then gathered it up and stowed it away in his luggage. He picked up the brochure and studied the photograph on its cover: an extraordinarily beautiful woman in an equally extraordinary gown. The caption read: "Alessandra Edel as Lady Macbeth."

Keyes sighed aloud and closed his eyes, then took a small, black hardcover notebook from the breast pocket of his jacket, and a pen. He flipped through the pages until he found one blank, scribbled for a moment, then sighed again.

"Don't get wound up, Claude," he mumbled to himself, "it's different now..."

I'm no longer an actor, he thought, and I am no longer a drunk... this time, Stratford will be different. He gave the woman on the brochure another glance. No, *everything* had not changed. Some things were more difficult to get over than others...

A hollow, echoing voice overhead announced the arrival of his train, first in English, then in French. Keyes stood, gathering together luggage and overcoat, and joined the boarding line-up at the gate.

Soon he was seated in a tiny smoking section on the train, staring out the window and moving toward his past.

ACT ONE

Dark on Monday

I shall tell you
A pretty tale; it may be you have heard it...
– *Coriolanus*, Act I, Scene 1

(1:1) A street corner in Stratford; the air is heavy with impending storm

FIRST WOMAN
There— across the street, waiting for the light to change... an example of exactly what I've been trying to explain to you.

SECOND WOMAN
You mean the one in the pink mini-skirt?

FIRST WOMAN
Yes; her legs are far too short for that skirt, and I mean, really— she jiggles standing still! That poor child isn't a fashion statement— she's a cry for help...

SECOND WOMAN
She doesn't look that bad to me...

FIRST WOMAN
She would if you'd been paying attention to me at all. Her make-up belongs on a Kabuki player and her clothes on a hooker!

SECOND WOMAN
Maybe she is a hooker...

FIRST WOMAN
Then she should at least try to appear expensive.

SECOND WOMAN
She's coming in our direction! Don't stare—

FIRST WOMAN
Why not? Looking isn't a crime.

THIRD WOMAN
Why don't you take a fucking Polaroid— it'll last longer!

From the notebook of Jean-Claude Keyes:

It's funny– during the two hours of the train trip between Toronto and Stratford, not once did I think about the Thomas Wolfe ramifications of this journey... (Come on, Keyes– Stratford, the theatre... they were never "home." They were just places you worked once. Worked... fell in love... fell down occasionally– maybe it *was* home, after all.) But, for the first few minutes after getting off the train, I saw the town through younger eyes, the eyes of a fledgling actor, full of ambition, of theory and dream... full of gold-plated horseshit, O'Reilly would say.

I find, somewhat to my surprise, that I am glad to be back in Stratford, with its parks and restaurants and eager-to-please shopkeepers whose mission in life is to sell me those wonderful souvenirs without which the Stratford experience is incomplete.

Stratford, and the Shakespearean Festival: to some (young actors, for example), it is the place where listless bank accounts may be raised up and made hale again, to fuel the rest of the year, when normally, to work in the arts in Canada is to live in a poverty that makes church-mice seem affluent.

Stratford... gold... The story of King Midas never mentions if he ever turned shit into gold, but that alchemy is often attempted in Stratford's theatres, and, often, the thaumaturgy fails. But when it succeeds, when the gold flows, when the lights fade and wonder really does return to the world for three hours or so, then the misfires and bombs are worth it, redeemed by gold. That promise is what brought me here once before, as participant, and I guess it's the same promise that's partially responsible for my returning as a civilian— to find that perfect theatrical moment.

I have high hopes for that moment's occurrence in this week's offerings, especially in *The Tempest.* Most of the elements are right: the casting, the support staff... and the few elements that are wrong— the smirking gargoyles who slip through the net, ready to repaint the cathedral into a K-Mart— are not insoluble problems; two sticks of dynamite or a couple of well-placed silver bullets should do the trick. Or maybe just leave the villains standing out in the November rain, to shrivel up like the Wicked Witch of the West. A storm started as my train pulled out of Toronto, and it looks like it might rain all week...

Among the many things I find unchanged is the pub I loved so much in the old days; it's bigger, and has had a fresh coat of paint, but my favourite table is still here— the table that always had only one chair, which discouraged company during those times when I needed to be alone to run my lines or nurse my hangovers.

I feel as if I am in a revival of some play I toured with once.

And, Sandra is somewhere in Stratford, again—

(1:2) The Jester's Bells, a pub in Stratford, Ontario

The Jester's Bells, or The Balls as it was frequently called by its regulars, was a dismal place in the afternoon if there were matinée performances in the theatres. The tourists, indeed theatre-goers of all sorts, were doing what they were meant to be doing– they were theatre-going. Similarly, the actors were acting, the stage-crews crewing, the dressers dressing, the managers managing.

The pub was almost empty. A man lazily wiped down the bar's dark wood with a damp white cloth. A scullion in the kitchen was ordering the chaos left there by luncheon. A waitress named Julia dreamed over coffee about next season's casting and the fine role she would have at last– one of the Three Sisters, she thought, or something contemporary. Shakespearean diction was not her strong suit, even if Shakespearean costumes with their tight bodices were.

Jean-Claude Keyes, plain "Claude" to most of his Anglo-Canadian friends, was in the process of deciding whether to imbue Julia with dubious immortality by describing her spiky brown hair and perfect ankles in his notebook, when he heard his name called from the other end of the room, which was a considerable distance. The Bells was a vast space, divided into two discrete areas by the bar itself; one side was primarily for dining, the other for drinking and carousing. Keyes was in the latter.

"Jon-Clod, you bastard!" howled a deep and commanding voice from the outer reaches of the pub, and Seamus

O'Reilly was upon Keyes before he could find refuge. Keyes smiled– the big old Irish son of a bitch was carrying his own chair! So much for cleverness and subterfuge...

Had it been anyone else, Keyes would most probably have ignored him or her at least long enough to finish making his notebook entry, but you did not ignore Seamus O'Reilly any more than you ignored earthquake, fire, flood or famine; in any case, Keyes thought, ignoring the subject of the biography Keyes was writing was probably unwise.

O'Reilly was neither so deep as a well nor so wide as a church door, but he was enough and served no one but himself. The red hair was greying, but tufts of flame remained to caution the unwary, and his six foot three bulk showed no signs of bending or breaking, although Keyes knew him to be some years over sixty. There were, to be sure, signs of fraying around the edges, such as the paunched belly and the reading glasses, but somehow O'Reilly managed to carry such things as badges of courage and honour. And, Keyes admitted to himself, he was glad to see the old fraud.

"You're in *my* spot!" O'Reilly announced, placing his chair and himself under his favourite panel in the extraordinary mural paintings that were the principal decoration of The Jester's Bells. In the passage that O'Reilly favoured, a giantess reclined in voluptuous languor. The old actor's shaggy head appeared to lie almost in her lap, which was the way he liked it. He set before him on the table a jigger-glass that had recently contained Bushmill's Irish whiskey. Beside it rose a pint of Guinness, at which he nibbled from time to time.

"Hello, Seamus," Keyes said."I was planning on calling you a little later. How have you been?"

"Since when do you give a tinker's tit, you cowardly disgrace to the profession? All you're worried about is that I live long enough for you to get everything you need for your damned book! And that I *will* die as soon as you've finished it so you don't have to pay me... What's that– ginger-ale? Drink for cub scouts!" The big head lifted and swung about like a gun turret in search of something to blow out of the water. His melodramatic eyes fixed on the waitress.

"Julia!" he bellowed, and his fingers snapped beneath the table with an explosive report that almost knocked the poor dreamer off her chair.

"What?" said the waitress, looking frantically around; she had been a tad slow in bringing Keyes his pitiful soft drink earlier, but arrived now as if on roller-blades almost before O'Reilly had finished his Celtic war-cry, looking for all the world like a handmaiden breathless with the honour of providing libations for some deity. O'Reilly was many things, Keyes thought, but not one of those things was *small*; and the world he magnanimously allowed to surround him had bloody well better realize that fact.

"Yes, sir. Do you want something from the bar?"

"Madam, I do," O'Reilly intoned in the ironical voice that he usually reserved for the sinister roles: Creon, Claudius, or Cenci. "Two Bushmill's, if you would be so very kind."

The head bartender, Bruno by name, was more watchful than his assistant or his waitress, and had the drinks ready on the bar. Bruno was a tall lean man of indeterminate age and angular features. The bones in his face seemed almost to have been honed to their sharpness. It was a piratical face, the face of a Breton filibustier of the seventeenth century or a Chicago gangster of the Roaring Twenties.

Julia picked up the drinks, and took a moment arranging them on her tray while she got into character, then returned to her customers.

"There you go," she crooned. "Enjoy."

O'Reilly half-bowed with a fragment of good humour.

"Madam, we shall do our best to 'enjoy,' but in this age of betrayals..."

Keyes laughed. "This what? Betrayals?"

O'Reilly scowled, downed his whiskey, sipped his Guinness, then stared at the drink he had purchased for Keyes as if a full glass was some kind of Satanist abomination.

"Well?!" he said, lowering his voice to a decibel or two below a full orchestra. "Are you going to drink that, or write about it?"

Keyes took a small sip, then a slightly larger one, as a knot of young actors came through the door. Each smiled toward O'Reilly, heads all but bowed in reverence... except for the dark-haired, lithe, grinning man who brought up the rear. He made a point of *not* acknowledging the Grand Old Man of Stratford. O'Reilly himself seemed to have missed the bravado performance, but Keyes knew better.

"What'd you do to *that* kid?" he asked. "Steal his lunch-money, or his girl?"

O'Reilly glared at Keyes, glared his most tyrannical glare, the one he reserved for his great roles, or his Great Roles, as he tended to think of them: Oedipus, Tamerlane, Lear...

Then he rolled his eyes toward the ceiling, as if Keyes' words were rapiers piercing him, or the daggers of a pack of conspirators.

Keyes was amused by his preposterous friend, and intrigued.

"Come on, Seamus. What's going on?"

"I don't want to discuss it."

"Sure you do."

O'Reilly filled his mouth and gullet with Guinness, then wiped foam from his moustache.

"*Him*," he said, inclining his head after the disrespectful young man. "That troglodyte, Alan Wales. Some evening– some evening soon, I suspect– I shall have to tear him limb from limb."

"As bad as that, is it?"

"Worse. I shall have to rip him from his guggle to his zatch."

"Wales has a zatch?"

O'Reilly grinned wickedly, nodded wisely. "Oh, he has a zatch all right... for the time being... but soon... soon, when I get through with him..."

"What did he do?" Keyes persisted. "Upstage you?"

O'Reilly grew in his chair, swelling visibly into a creature almost twice the size he had been only seconds before. He also changed colour, or at least his face did. It went from the fine healthy red of freshly cut beef-steak to the empurpled ox-blood of old field boots.

"Upstage me!" he roared. "*Me?*"

Keyes retreated from this unwise suggestion as rapidly as possible.

"Sorry. How could I have imagined anything so stupid?"

"How indeed?" The colour of O'Reilly's face remained fierce.

"I said I was sorry. What did he do?"

"He tried– *tried*, mind you– to upstage me, but it's not for a trifle like that I intend to draw and neatly quarter him. Ha!"

"I see," Keyes said. His voice was grave now, as full of concern as if he were listening to a tale of atrocity, lynching, or mass murder. "When did all this happen?"

"When? It happens every time that swivel-arsed cannibal is allowed onstage, most foully in *Twelfth Night!*"

"I haven't seen it yet."

"It had a chance... oh, yes, an excellent chance. It might have been the best of all the Stratford *Twelfth Nights*, of all the century's *Twelfth Nights*. It might have been superb. My Sir Toby, if I do say so..."

"I've been looking forward to seeing it," insisted Keyes, which was true enough.

"Forget it," the old actor groaned. "He's ruined the play. He's pulled it all down into a shambles... shambles..."

"He plays Sebastian?"

"Sebastian? Good Lord, no. A Sebastian might almost get away with dancing about like a go-go girl..."

Keyes giggled. "A go-go girl? I haven't heard that expression since I was a kid."

"Scratching his arm-pit," O'Reilly continued, "adjusting his crotch..."

"Not Orsino, surely."

O'Reilly frowned as if Keyes were being purposely very stupid or obtuse.

"No, not Orsino," he said with a patient look that was exaggerated almost to saintliness. O'Reilly was used to playing across footlights. Even his small expressions were larger than life. "He's cast as Feste. I have no idea what he's playing, nor does he. He's wriggling his arse, that's all."

"That has been done before..." Keyes mused. "But Feste? I haven't seen the play in years... since *I* played Orsino, as a matter of fact. You think Feste is important?"

"Important? The action depends absolutely on Feste."

"Does it?"

"He's the one who understands, you see," O'Reilly explained. "The only one who understands everything."

"But he's a clown."

"Exactly... the supreme clown. What's *Twelfth Night* about?"

It was Keyes' turn to frown. "I said I haven't seen it recently."

"It's about love, you twit. It's about physical, sexual love."

"You say that about all the plays, Seamus."

"And I'm right, Claude... most of the time, anyway." He finished his drink and glanced toward the waitress. This time Julia was ready for him.

"Two more," she said, right on cue.

"Not for me," Keyes said. "It's the middle of the afternoon."

"What's that got to do with anything?" O'Reilly said.

"Aren't you playing tonight?"

"I am and I shall. Tonight is not this afternoon." He looked again at the waiting waitress. "Just one, please, Madam. My cousin is not well."

Julia nodded and retreated.

"I still don't get it. About Feste, I mean."

"I will make everything clear as soon as my cup is refreshed," O'Reilly said. He leaned back in his chair to stare at the ceiling until this condition had been fulfilled. Upon the waitress' return, O'Reilly scooped the tiny glass directly from her tray into his large fist and sipped a sixteenth of an inch of liquid off the top of it.

"Ah..." he looked soulfully at Julia. "Thank you, my dear Hebe. You may withdraw."

She hesitated. "Should I run a tab?"

"By all means," O'Reilly said. "Run..." he rolled the 'R' mightily, "Run... a tab."

"No problem," she said, and exited, scribbling.

"Where was I?"

"Feste?" Keyes suggested.

"Love," O'Reilly corrected. "Everybody in the play is in love."

"Everybody?"

"Think about it."

But Keyes didn't have to think about it because O'Reilly launched immediately into an explication of the text.

"Orsino loves Olivia, right?"

"Ye...es."

"Of course he does. That's all he talks about. And Olivia, too, is in love. Not with Orsino, the poor sod, but with her brother, then with Cesario, and finally with Sebastian."

"I really don't remember..."

"You don't need to. Just listen. Antonio also loves Sebastian..."

"Antonio?" Keyes put in timidly. He could remember Antonios in Shakespeare, but not an Antonio in *Twelfth Night*.

"Shut up and pay attention. Cesario, who is Viola in drag, loves Orsino. Malvolio loves Olivia, but not so much as he loves himself. Maria loves Sir Toby, and so does that silly ass Sir Andrew in his witless way. Sir Toby loves cakes and ale, or rather ale and cakes, and does so with a constancy that few men lavish on their ladies."

"Seamus, I..." Keyes peeked at his watch.

"Never mind the time. I'm just getting to the point of all this; only Feste is not in love. Feste is Eros-proof, because Feste is a Fool, and it is a Fool's high and lonely responsibility to be unlike the people around him. Like those mirrors in carnival shows, Feste must twist the other players, must distort their images, invert them... And do you know why?"

Keyes shook his head.

O'Reilly reached across the table and caught hold of his friend's wrist.

"He does it to reveal the Truth." A great grin of satisfaction spread across the actor's time-rumpled face. "The Truth!"

"The truth," Keyes echoed. Trapped, he saw that he might as well help O'Reilly's argument to a hasty end. "And you think Wales isn't doing that, revealing the truth, I mean."

"He's revealing only his arse. He hasn't the foggiest notion of what the part is about, or what acting is about, or..."

"And the director? Does he feel the way you do?"

"He must," O'Reilly said. "Porliss is pompous, but he's not stupid. I think Wales must have something on him."

"I'm not sure I agree with you about Hobart Porliss' intelligence... Blackmail, you think?"

"Why not? Wales wouldn't be the first whore to try it."

Not until this moment did Keyes realize how serious his old friend was. He was used to O'Reilly's exaggeration, but his shift of tone to simple candour startled Keyes.

"You really mean it, don't you? You hate this kid."

"You are too modest, sir," O'Reilly said, returning to his more familiar and expansive manner. "I loathe him, despise him, execrate him..."

"Okay, okay," Keyes said, breaking in on O'Reilly's rage. "Alan Wales has ruined *Twelfth Night* for you."

O'Reilly shook his head. "Not for me, Cousin. Just say that he has ruined *Twelfth Night.*"

He said these last words softly and with great feeling, as if he were speaking of a desecration, an altar bespoiled or a temple pulled down. O'Reilly was The Real Thing, an actor who lived for his art and doubtless would die for it, or because of it, or both. For the first time Keyes suspected that O'Reilly might almost kill for it.

"It's atrocious," O'Reilly said, "to use a part like that just to get somebody to look at your arse."

"Seamus, I think we should..."

"To make matters worse, the dim-witted Anthropophagus can't sing."

"Sing?" Keyes said.

"You *have* been away a long time, haven't you? Feste has to sing. The Fool's part is full of songs."

"I do remember, now." Rather tunelessly, Keyes brought forth a line to prove it: "For the rain it raineth every day..."

"That's right," O'Reilly said, "except you, bad as you are, are better than Wales– he runs off at the mouth like a sewage sandwich." Then he threw back his head, opened his mouth wide, and in his big warm baritone, sang:

Come away, come away, death,
And in sad cypress let me be laid;
Fly away, fly away, breath...

Keyes got to his feet, put a five dollar bill on the table. "I've got to go. Take it easy, Seamus. There's always next year."

O'Reilly seemed not to notice the money. He stared into his glass, which was empty again.

"That's for my whiskey," Keyes said.

The old actor nodded. "Next year, you say."

"Sure. There'll be other plays. There will probably be other *Twelfth Nights* for you, and other Sir Tobys as well. Not next year maybe..." Keyes was aware of how feeble it sounded.

"More Sir Tobys you think, do you?"

"I don't like seeing you so grim."

"Thank you, Claude, but grim is how I feel. Fare thee well, Cousin."

Keyes hesitated a moment, then turned and made his way down the aisle between the bar and tables, toward the back door. He could heard O'Reilly's big voice behind him, again singing one of Feste's songs:

My shroud of white, stuck all with yew,
O, prepare it!
Not a flower, not a flower sweet,
On my black coffin let there be strown;
Not a friend, not a friend greet
My poor corpse, where my bones
Shall be thrown...

Unfortunately, his friend's aria was abruptly drowned out by raucous, donkey-like laughter from the section of the pub which Keyes was passing, marked off by partitions and waist-high railings, for the playing of darts. The voices belonged to young and cocky men, among them the arse-twitching Alan Wales.

Keyes was somewhat shocked to see Wales raise a hand and fling at the dartboard, not a dart, but a bone-handled hunting knife. It struck the bullseye with a loud *thunk* and quivered in the cork, dwarfing the other, smaller missiles.

Keyes glanced toward the bartender, who shook his head in disgust, but made no move to interfere with or censure Wales' unsportsmanlike and dangerous violation of the rules of the game. Evidently it was still true, as it had been in Keyes' own day, that actors enjoyed a degree of licence in Stratford not granted to ordinary citizens. It was acknowledged by all, if sometimes grudgingly, that they were a breed apart, entitled on occasion to special treatment.

After all, the city's tourist-based economy depended on them.

(1:3) The home of Betty Beardsley, a Bed & Breakfast

Keyes was uncomfortably aware of how little booze it took to make him drunk these days as he did a slow, stately saunter along Ontario Street in the lessening rain. At this careful pace, it took him twenty minutes, rather than the usual ten, to reach Betty Beardsley's Bed & Breakfast.

This was in a house of the variety known in Stratford as a Queen Anne's Box, presumably because of the vaguely classical pediment on its gable. There were of course other interpretations for the label, some of which were quite rude. A large verandah had been wrapped about the front of the B & B in the decade before the First World War. A balcony had sprung up on the roof of this porch in the decade after. The latest renovation, executed by Betty herself, was one which amused Keyes, though several of her more conservative neighbours had complained: the original sedate brick was painted a dazzling yellow, and most of the wooden trim done in an equally bright blue.

Keyes came upon his hostess in the front foyer. Betty Beardsley stopped fussily straightening pictures to look at her guest, then sighed a sigh so heavy that a casual witness could be forgiven for inferring that she had just received news of immense import, perhaps direct from the oracle at Delphi. Betty was thin and bony to a point just short of emaciation. She had, in Keyes' opinion, an elegant face, a creased gauntness set off by a shaggy thatch of prematurely white hair.

There was almost always a cigarette between her lips and a drink of something close to hand.

"Well," she said, "don't *you* look stunning– just about as charming as this hall... but that's what I get for decorating it pissed! What should I do, Claude? Re-paint? Re-paper? Or just sell the whole damned thing and be done with it!"

"Whatever keeps you out of the pool hall, Betty. How's the new mural coming?"

"Fucking terribly, thank you! I'd advise to you keep out of my way– I'm in an unholy mood, so don't do anything to irritate me; don't even sneeze!"

"Don't worry– I'll be quiet as a mime troop with laryngitis. Tonight before the show I intend to have a drink, a hot bath, and several fantasies of times past, specifically about Goldie Semple in *Cat on a Hot Tin Roof*."

"In your dreams!"

"Exactly– best place in the world to find gold of any kind."

"You're a strange man, Keyes, even in the circle of friends *I* keep," Betty said, as she took down a reproduction– a fifteenth century St. Sebastian with too many arrows– sneered at it, then moved it to a spot on the far wall, beside one of her own works; it looked just as bad there. She stood back to stare at it. "Why did I buy this thing?"

"Probably because it was cheap," Keyes observed as he mounted the stairs leading to his room, leaving Betty to cuss elaborately about the insufferability of paying guests.

Keyes reached the pleasant little room which currently served him as home– it was painted a soft blue-grey, with matching draperies of a slightly darker hue; the furnishings were typical of a certain kind of Stratford B & B: garage-sale or auction specials, but only in the best of condition and in good taste. Here and there were small *objets d'art* of the same stamp. There was also something which had not been there this morning, Keyes discovered quite painfully with the big toe of his right foot: a heavy doorstop, the hostess' solution to a door that refused to remain open when room-airing time came about.

Keyes reached down to grab his injured toe, and cursed the offending object. And the small and consummately ugly cast iron bust of the Bard himself did offend.

Below, Betty heard the *thump* of contact and the stifled cry of pain and outrage; she came bounding up the stairs to see what had been broken.

"Oh," she said, quickly assessing the situation. "I see you found Mr. Shakespeare. He came in a box of junk I bought this morning at the auction– I was after a half-dozen old prints, but had to take the whole selection. Hideous, isn't it?"

"Hideous is a very small word for what that thing is," the victim replied, massaging his toe while hopping about on one foot like a great blue heron.

"Don't sue," said Betty. "I can't afford it."

"I'd like to sue whoever made that thing!"

"Don't worry about it– I'm sure there's a special circle of Hell for people who commit bad art..."

Keyes grinned an evil grin. "You'd better hope not!"

"Your rent for this week just doubled," Betty announced as she exited, pursued by laughter.

Keyes stretched out on the bed for a nap before dinner. He had an eight o'clock performance of *Julius Caesar* to attend. With Hermes Ziemski-Trapp directing, Keyes knew the play had every chance of being a long and tedious haul. He needed a brief lie-down beforehand, perhaps a decent erotic dream or two.

He got neither. Rather, he tossed and turned the whole time, and dreamed he was back carrying a spear in one of the *Henrys*. In the dream, he had forgotten to put on his costume and was standing shivering onstage, totally naked. Moreover, it was Keyes as he was now, thin and gone to seed rather than the well-muscled young actor he had been. The audience was filled with his fellow actors, as well as directors and designers, pages, attendants...

In the front row was the ghost of Banquo, laughing his ectoplasmic head off. Keyes wanted to tell the spirit that it was in the wrong play, but found that, besides being naked, he had forgotten his only line.

From the notebook of Jean-Claude Keyes:

Poor Betty... for all I torment her, I know she considers me a small curse compared to some who have passed through her Bed & Breakfast. Her first tourist guests, she once told me, were a pair of gay midgets– they had been far from boring, but hadn't paid their bill either. At least I do that much... and sometimes I'm not boring, either. Certainly my time here should be at least marginally exciting– not only am I here to visit and haunt old friends, but also to work on my book.

The theatrical career of my oldest friend, Seamus, has always seemed to me to be the stuff of modern legend, or at the very least, of modest biography, and my agent has convinced a publisher of the same. O'Reilly was very young in 1953, when he shared the stage, however briefly, with Alec Guinness in the opening season of this theatre. Since then– well, it will all be in my book, next year, by the grace of the gods and with the co-operation of Seamus O'Reilly. Most of my optimism rides on the former.

One of the most interesting things about O'Reilly is that he hates audiences; if a way could be found to run a theatre without them, he would dance with obscene joy. This was his main reason for once– unsuccessfully– attempting to work in American films. Certainly, the money had attracted him, as it had Lorne Greene, William Shatner, Kate Nelligan, and other Canadian actors, but more than anything it was the chance to do his job without dealing with the warm bodies in the front row– it made no difference to O'Reilly whether they loved or hated him; it was their presence alone he objected to.

Hollywood had been humiliating for him on so many levels that he refused even to go to movies any more. Just four years ago, Aubrey Barber had sought him out expressly to play the lead in a new film.

"You had your chance!" the great Canadian expatriate director had been told. "Now fuck off and leave me alone!" Garbo would have been proud.

And yet few suspected this of the man who had given them so many bravura Lears and Hamlets and even Romeos; audiences assumed he loved them as much as they loved him, that his purpose on the stages of the world was to delight them, to give them their money's worth. Both of these he did, but not by design. I believe he would play Othello in an empty barn to an audience of field mice– except that field mice don't buy the tickets which generate the salary that pays his bar tabs. I asked him once why he was an actor, and he quoted John Wayne: "A man's gotta do what a man's gotta do," which told me absolutely nothing.

Although the expression perhaps did explain my own situation, an intrinsically weird and potentially bloody one, to be sure. I had left the Festival company and the acting profession in an atmosphere of bitterness and hamstrung dreams. To return to it now, as biographer of one of its favourite sons and so by association of the Festival itself, is a somewhat delicate matter. The temperaments and the politics of the theatre business are as complex and dramatic as the plays themselves; my long and bumpy relationship with O'Reilly is no less complicated.

Preservation of both skin and integrity could turn out to be a highly complicated dance in which I will not even be allowed to lead, much less call the tune. And to think that I asked for this!

Perhaps my life would have been simpler had I settled for merely walking around the woods at the height of the hunting season wearing a deer suit... or if I had gone on CBC radio and insisted that the Prime Minister liked to put on his wife's underthings at Sunday dinner. But no, not me– instead I come, perhaps with band-aid in hand, to shake, if not to kiss, the bitten hand which once fondled me.

But, it's too late for any of this– I've set my stage, now I have to play on it. "You rip a' dese, you men a' dese!" as my old Classics prof used to say– she was a daffy old soul, for all of her genius.

(1:4) The Festival Theatre, balcony

Keyes was restless, uncomfortable, and just plain Bard-weary. In his time, he had seen more drama and depth in Walt Disney cartoons than in the *Julius Caesar* being dragged out on the thrust-stage below. For some reason unfathomable to Keyes, the action was set in a combination of modern-day America and Imperial Rome– the wondrous subtlety of symbolism, he supposed. Caesar seemed to be a kind of JFK figure in Roman drag. The senators wore togas, but carried briefcases (which in turn contained daggers), and sported mirror-style sunglasses as well. Various statues of Roman deities littered the stage, and the statues' faces were rough approximations of Nixon, Reagan, and one of them, he was sure, was Mikhail Gorbachev. What in the name of poetic licence was an audience to make of all that? And who cared? It was all too, too tedious.

In an effort to reduce at least his physical discomfort, Keyes stretched his long legs as far as the seating would allow, and was rewarded by a loud *crack* from his aching joints– not so loud as a gunshot, but loud enough; a quick glance assured him that no one had been disturbed by his knees' indiscretion. Perhaps everyone else in the audience was asleep– he certainly wished he was.

Keyes returned his attention with a great exercise of will to the so-called drama. He had not escaped unnoticed after all: Brutus himself was glaring in Keyes' direction.

The next scene was such a masterpiece of stagecraft that Keyes committed his second *faux pas* of the evening.

He yawned. Completely unintentionally to be sure, but his voice-projection was as good as it had ever been. There was a suppressed ripple of giggles from his immediate neighbours (the heartiest from others in the business), from two ushers, and from some poor soul onstage who would no doubt soon be looking for work at the Shaw Festival. That's it, Keyes thought, and under cover of a convenient blackout slipped from his aisle seat and headed for the nearest exit. When *he* was more entertaining than a multi-thousand dollar production, it was time to go. Anyway, he knew how the play ended. There was no sense subjecting himself to any more just to find out how many metaphors for "bomb" he could come up with. Oh, brave new world, that has such turkeys in it, he thought as he escaped, followed by a chorus of smirks and mimed applause.

Now he had an unplanned evening to kill, but luckily he also had a list of old friends and acquaintances yet to be blessed with the triumphant return of Jean-Claude Keyes to Stratford. Armed with notebook and quarters, he stalked and trapped the nearest pay-phone.

But his luck was running poorly. Those he called were either out working, drunk, or had prior engagements. He did however, manage to arrange a tea-time assignation for the following day with the leading lady of his cast of old friends, and of this year's Festival company as well. His face was lined with a curious blend of smile and frown as he hung up the phone.

(1:5) The apartment of Alessandra Edel

Alessandra Edel lived in one of the fine old Victorian houses which have survived in Stratford. Her apartment was on its top floor, close beneath a steep mansard roof.

"My garret," she was in the habit of saying at the drop of almost anybody's hat. This she would usually qualify with something like: "It's a shabby old place but I love it. It has the atmosphere I require for my work..."

Keyes got there at sundown. Sandra had given him instructions about finding his way through the house and up to her flat, instructions that were not at all clear.

"If you get lost," she said, "knock on a door and ask somebody. You speak the language of the natives."

After climbing a couple of stairways and groping his way along several gloomy corridors, Keyes did get lost. Behind one of the doors, someone was playing Rameau. He associated harpsichord music with a certain level of sophistication, perhaps of intelligence, so he tapped discreetly and waited patiently.

"Go away," a voice called above the strumming of *La Dauphine*. "Whatever it is, I don't want it."

Keyes was unsure about the gender of the voice– tenor? contralto? He decided not to try to find out. Instead, he groped further, found another staircase, another door. This one was opened by Sandra.

"My darling," she said in her fine voice. "Did you have trouble finding me?"

I always have, he thought, but confined himself to telling of his brief encounter with Rameau.

"Oh, that's the other tenant, Grace Lockhardt," Sandra informed him. "She's a dresser... my dresser actually. A nice girl, a bit flaky, but good at her job."

Then she kissed him, pulled him into her apartment, and poured him a cup of tea.

"Tell me everything," she said. "It's been such a long time."

Keyes didn't know what she meant by "everything," so he told her where he'd been and what he'd been doing for the past few years. As he told her, he thought his life didn't sound very amusing. Her face told him the same thing.

"But how interesting," Sandra lied. She lied several times as she refilled his teacup, and refilled it again. Her voice was low and world-weary. Even when Sandra was young, Keyes remembered, her voice had been like that, the voice of someone who had seen and done a lot, or rather more than a lot.

The day died without fanfare or applause while he was telling his story. No lamp had yet been lit. Deep shadow crowded the room. Only with difficulty could he make out the silhouette of Sandra's form in the darkness, that body which he remembered as vividly as he did her face. She was an audible presence still, an emanation, but nothing more substantial.

Perhaps to demonstrate her palpable existence, Sandra shifted in her chair. Shadows prevented Keyes from seeing this movement clearly, but he heard the groan of a leather belt, the rattle of a chain, the hiss of silk or some other smooth fabric over even smoother flesh. They were sounds he interpreted as being signals, although he was not sure of what.

She made another movement, this time with her hand.

"The place is a bit of a mess," she apologized not very sincerely.

"I'm used to a bit of mess in this life," he said.

"This is Sheila Tarleton's apartment actually," Sandra continued. "She's in Toronto, playing a mid-wife or something in a dreadful television thing. The money is excellent of course, but they're shooting part of it in Kapuskasing."

Keyes had no idea who Sheila Tarleton was, but that made no difference to Sandra. She assumed that he would know the people she knew, or at least that he would care to know these people. Are they all like that? he wondered, theatre people? Indifferent to all other worlds but their own? Was I like that? Is that one of the reasons I gave it up?

For a while they sat in the gloom saying nothing, then Keyes heard the groan of leather again, and the hiss of silk, as Sandra got to her feet.

"How did it get to be so late?"

She said it less to him than to herself, or to the murk about her. She put on a light, but it barely brightened the room; its shade was draped with the coloured cloth of a scarf too frayed to wear.

Keyes surveyed the apartment. Its living room, where they were having their tea, looked more like a prop-room than a salon. There wasn't much furniture but the space was crowded with things: hat boxes, umbrellas, boots, pictures, and other odds and ends, including a candelabrum seven feet tall, a cello, some moribund plants, and what once may have been a *papier mâché* bull.

"If I had known you were going to be in town, I would have tried to make the place more presentable."

Keyes knew this to be patently untrue. Sandra had on occasion lived in "presentable" quarters, but she had never kept them that way herself.

"I wasn't sure when I was coming," he said, "not until a couple of weeks ago."

Sandra wandered away to light other lamps. This activity, so daily and banal, became a performance as she did it, a sort of ritual, a slow stately progress from one beacon to the next.

Watching her, Keyes remembered the woman she had been when they were lovers. He found her very little changed. She had aged of course, but not unpleasantly. A few grey strands filigrained her auburn hair. She was heavier, her shoulders thicker and her hips more ample, but she had always been large– broad and thick and powerful. Her bosom, he thought, seemed less aggressive to him now.

Necessarily this close investigation of her person made him remember other parts of her as well, parts he could not see. He remembered too the uses he had made of them, and she of him, the intimacies they had shared.

"How long has it been?" Sandra asked, breaking in on his thoughts from the far end of the room.

He surprised himself by knowing almost to the day, or night, as was in fact the case.

"It'll be fifteen years," he said, "next month..."

For a moment she looked puzzled, then she smiled the bittersweet smile for which she had once been famous.

"I only meant how long since you were last in Stratford. You haven't changed much, darling."

"I guess not," Keyes said, trying to laugh, "not as far as you're concerned, anyway."

Her smile faded. Almost solemnly they looked at one another across the distance separating them. Then, abruptly, Sandra crossed to one of the room's big dormer windows. She paused there– posed there, Keyes thought– dramatically framed by the night.

"Don't you want to hear about my work?" Her tone was ironic, almost jeering.

"Lady Macbeth, you mean. That's marvellous."

"Yes, I'm pleased about that, especially since the cast is good and for once Porliss seems to know what he's doing. But this is a repertory company, darling. I'm also playing Juliet's nurse."

Keyes started to say something, but thought better of it.

"Careful, darling," Sandra said ominously. "Don't tell me that Juliet's nurse is a good part, an interesting role, and all that. It's a bore, and worse, an elephant's graveyard for elderly actresses."

"Oh, come on, Sandra, you know better than that. The role takes maturity but..."

"The finest nurse I ever saw was done by a gay actor who was still in his twenties. Danny Fleet. Do you remember him? He had the time of his life."

Keyes didn't remember.

Sandra shrugged, massively. "It's a bore. But that's the way I'm cast these days– if I'm cast at all."

"Still, Lady Macbeth..."

"Don't try to make me feel good. I hate it when people try to make me feel good."

She fixed him with a severe look while she tried to decide how much she hated being made to feel good. Then her mood changed again. She shook her head and launched into a description of the *Romeo and Juliet*– the *R and J*, as she called it. She spoke angrily, grumbling grandly and often, but through it all Keyes could hear the enthusiasm, the passion for play-acting, for putting on a show, that he remembered so well from the part of her past he had shared. She swung her head away and stared out the window, offering him as she did her right profile, always her finest aspect. A siren howled in the distance, came closer, passed not far from the house, then faded into nothingness across the river– an ambulance on its way to the General Hospital. Still Sandra gazed out into the night. She seemed to have forgotten that Keyes was there.

Brooding, he thought, the way she used to. He knew better than to interrupt her when she was like this, so he made use of the gap in conversation to look about the room again, especially at the walls which were hung with theatrical memorabilia: costume drawings, programs, playbills– works from the Sheila Tarleton collection, he presumed.

One poster, however, surely belonged to Sandra. It had a battered frame and fingerprints on the glass. No doubt she travelled with it, took it along whenever she moved, which was often. Keyes knew it was hers because he remembered the play it advertised.

THE WHITE DEVIL
The Life and Death of Vittoria Corombona
Courtesan of Venice

Sandra's name was there, too, and in larger type than any of the other actors':

ALESSANDRA EDEL

Keyes looked again at her, remembering her most successful role. Could she, he wondered, still play the villainous Vittoria Corombona? It was not exactly a part for a girl, after all. With some good clothes she might manage it, proper make-up, a clever lighting designer...

Sandra must have felt his eyes upon her.

"Can you think of any reason," she asked, as if there had been no break in their dialogue, "why we shouldn't have a drink?"

Without waiting for an answer, she set off for the kitchen. On the way she passed close to him, brushing his leg with her skirt, touching his shoulder affectionately with her hand.

When she came back, she had a green-black bottle in one hand and two crystal flutes in the other.

"I get tired of Shakespeare sometimes," she said, "and even of Racine, but I never get tired of champagne."

Keyes considered offering to help with the cork, but thought better of it, which was just as well since Sandra opened the bottle far more deftly than he probably would have done. She filled their glasses just as proficiently.

"Chateau Mandragora!" she said with a certain muted gaiety.

They drank, and drank deeply. An hour later they were drinking still, although no longer from the first bottle– drinking and talking. All the uneasiness between them had disappeared. Only a lovely sort of tension remained, for Keyes at least, an edge of expectancy, the function of questions yet to be asked and answers fervently desired. He was about to attempt the first of these when Sandra suddenly rose and left the room.

"We'd better have something to eat," she called over her shoulder as she went.

The tray she brought back was loaded with dishes of this and that, nothing that could be called a meal, but random delicatessen.

"I rarely cook nowadays," she explained, setting the tray on a table near Keyes.

He could not remember that she ever had, but he was careful not to say so.

"You don't have the time," he murmured.

"Actually I often have too much time, but that was well said, my gracious lord." Her voice changed in the middle of the sentence, became that of the old-fashioned Shakespearean player, fruity and affected. "Although the fare be poor, 'twill fill our stomachs– please you eat of it."

Keyes helped himself to a slice of smoked salmon and a wedge of lemon.

"Lemons," he said dreamily, "lemons..."

He thought for a moment, then tried his own remnant of a stage voice. "Ah, Flaminia! Your lemons!"

Sandra looked pleased, almost tender.

"You remember that?" she said softly.

"The Goldoni? Of course I do. You were terrific."

"It's an odd thing to remember."

"You were terrific," he insisted.

She needed no further prompting, then quite miraculously, it seemed to Keyes (despite his own knowledge of the craft of acting), she was transformed. Sandra was gone; Alessandra Edel was gone. In her place stood Flaminia, the *soubrette* of the Commedia dell' Arte– leering, bawdy Flaminia, gesturing extravagantly, hopping from one foot to the other, thrusting out her breasts, grinding her pelvis...

"And your meat, Arlecchino!" she crowed, making the name itself sound lewd. "Dear Arlecchino!"

Keyes clapped, and clamoured for more.

She laughed, bowed, and sank into a chaise longue. "That makes me feel almost young."

She reached for her glass. They drank again, then returned to talking of the theatre, or Sandra's corner of it anyway. Other parts she had played were evoked, especially those from her early years. She reminisced about her Charmian, her Maeve, her Amala, her Pirate Jenny. They even talked about her Vittoria.

"You were never better," Keyes said, "than as Vittoria."

She said nothing but he could see that this pleased her.

"You should do it again. Someone should revive it for you."

She looked at him as if he were a child, fondly but from a great height.

"Are you serious? *The White Devil*? Who would do a play like that? Most directors don't even know it."

"Why not? It's famous enough– a classic, as they say."

She laughed. "You *have* been away, haven't you, darling? You hang out in libraries, but directors don't. Directors don't read. They just attend plays done by other directors, then do the plays again in different places."

"Like *Romeo and Juliet*."

"Exactly."

She drained her glass and turned again to the window, looked out at the towers of her neighbourhood's old houses. They talked less about the stage after that, more about themselves, about the things they had done together.

"Do you remember the day we went to...?"

"Do you remember the party at...?"

"Do you remember the night...?"

"What's become of Grazia?"

"Have you heard anything from Edward?"

"Where do you suppose Daphne is?"

"Where's Boris?"

"David?"

"Caroline?"

"Fitz?"

Eventually they reached that point in the evening when Keyes boozily came to the conclusion that the script required him to suggest they go to bed together.

"It'll be like old times," he said.

There was a solemn moment. Sandra looked at Keyes, appraising him almost as if she were sober. Then she cast a quick glance at a small gilt frame. Keyes followed her gaze with his own. A very pretty face grinned from the frame, the face of the dark-haired young actor O'Reilly disliked so much, Alan Wales.

"I don't think so, darling," Sandra said at last. "Nothing else is like old times."

Keyes was not so drunk that he failed to see the truth in what she said.

"There's someone else," he said after a moment of foggy rumination.

Sandra nodded. "There's always someone else, isn't there?"

"I suppose there is, one way or another," he agreed sadly. Then he struggled to his feet, kissed her almost paternally on the forehead.

"In that case I must go to bed alone," he said, trying to make it sound easy.

Keyes moved off toward the door. When he got there he turned and looked back.

"You should turn in, too," he said in a proprietary voice that echoed back to their years of cohabitation. "You must be as bushed as I am."

"Do I look... bushed?"

Drunk as he was, Keyes avoided the trap and managed a final gallantry: "You look splendid!"

"Of course I do. Now run along. I've got to think about Juliet's nurse."

She rummaged through a heap of books and papers on the floor beside the chaise longue until she found a script. Without looking his way again, she opened it and began to read.

Keyes left her to her script. He turned, stumbled, and fell heavily among the hat boxes.

Sandra was beside him before he could get up. "You're drunk, darling. Did you hurt yourself?"

He hadn't, but he had made such a spectacle of himself that Sandra refused to let him leave.

"There's a bed in the little room, darling. You have a nap and then you can go home."

Keyes did as he was told. Because of the wine he fell immediately asleep. Also because of the wine he did not stay asleep. Less than an hour after he lay down, he was up again, suffering from a terrible thirst. He went into the hall. Somewhere, he told himself, there has to be a kitchen, and in it the solace of cool, clear water.

But before he found the kitchen, he came to the door of the room in which he had left Sandra. At the bottom of that door there was a ribbon of light, faint and roseate. A lamp had been left burning in the big room.

How like her, he thought, to forget the lights. She still needs a keeper, or a slave.

He was about to go inside and tidy up after her, as he had done often enough in the past, when he was stopped by the sound of her voice.

"... Do thy office in right form," he heard Sandra say, although the words coming through the door were muffled and imprecise.

Juliet's nurse, Keyes told himself, she's still working on her lines. He put his shoulder to the door and pushed it open.

Once again Sandra was beside the window looking out into the night. She had changed her clothes. Now she wore a dress of dark velvet, which Keyes took to be a nightgown, until he saw how elaborately it was cut– high-bodiced, full-skirted, with padded shoulders and slashed sleeves. She was wearing a Renaissance dress in fact, or some stage person's idea of one.

She had changed her hair as well, put it up in coils and braids, fixed it with bright-headed pins and fancy combs. Jewels gleamed at her throat, on her hands, her wrists.

"I am too true a woman," she said, her voice smouldering. "Conceit can never kill me..."

With the door ajar, he could hear her perfectly. Her voice was so full, so perfectly controlled that it seemed operatic. It was a voice for playing high tragedy, or high melodrama.

Juliet's nurse? Keyes asked himself, knowing that it could not be.

"I will not in my death shed one base tear. Or if look pale, for want of blood, not fear..."

At last he knew. Of course it wasn't Juliet's nurse there by the window. It was Vittoria Corombona. Sandra was staging her own revival of *The White Devil*, playing it with all her heart to the night, or to the lights of Stratford, those that remained on at this late hour... lights that rose tier on tier like the loges in a theatre.

"My greatest sin lay in my blood: now my blood pays for it..."

With a burglar's stealth Keyes put out his hand and pulled the door toward him.

"My soul, like a ship in a black storm..."

The door closed silently, ending the performance– for Keyes at least. Once more he made his way along the corridor toward the kitchen. When he found it, he drank as deeply of water as earlier he had of champagne. Before he left the kitchen on his way home, he carefully tore a blank page from the back of his notebook, scribbled briefly on it, and left it on the counter.

You were never better, the note said. *Brava!*

From the notebook of Jean-Claude Keyes:

It's been some years since I had a hangover as memorable as the one precipitated by my reunion with Sandra– the last time was also in Stratford, on the night Sandra decided we should pursue our roles in life on separate stages.

Luckily, Stratford's layout is fairly congenial to children, fools, tourists, and drunks, since everything essential is about eight feet from everything else, and thus my journey homewards from Sandra's was not so fraught with terror as it might have been in Toronto, although I did almost fall in the river once. The police were nowhere in evidence, also to my benefit... I'm sure my tipsy state was as obvious as Mae West's libido.

It was good to see Sandra... and good to know she would forgive me my embarrassing behaviour– it isn't as if she hasn't seen me make an ass of myself before. And good to know we are still able to act like friends, in spite of the years, and her new lover.

Judging by my first few gin-soaked days, it seems that my friends and acquaintances remain loyal alumni of the Old School of alcohol consumption– the school run by the Marquis de Sade. It would probably be to my benefit to swear a mighty vow to earth and sky and ancestors to avoid those places and people that tempt me to strong drink: The Balls, O'Reilly, Sandra, Betty...

Fat chance.

ACT TWO

The Scottish Play

... look down into this den,
And see a fearful sight of blood and death...
– *Titus Andronicus*, Act II, Scene 3

(2:1) The Festival Theatre Marquee

The Festival Theatre is a sprawling building situated only a few blocks from downtown Stratford. The theatre's design echoes on a grander scale the tent in which the first season's plays were performed.

Extending along the rear of the Festival for some two hundred feet is the Marquee, an open-air deck on which receptions and other functions are held. The Marquee overlooks a hill that slopes gently down to a grass playing-field, the site of the annual cricket match between the Festival company and Niagara's Shaw Festival.

Looking up from the field, the tourist can see that directly under the Marquee is a stretch of plate-glass windows, running almost the entire length of the building. Behind these windows toil some of the theatre's invisible wizards, the prop-builders, the costume-makers. Where the windows end to the east, the wall sheers off at an angle, creating a small, sheltered alcove, overhung by a thin strip of the Marquee flooring.

On this overhang, Hobart Porliss, the director of the Scottish Play, and George Brocken, its designer, stood talking together, beside a circular hole in the deck, a well twelve or fifteen feet across, with, appropriately, a circular railing around it. The hole looked down approximately fifteen feet into the alcove. The well-hole above and the alcove below were rigged to allow actors to practice climbing rope-ladders from the ground level up to the Marquee. A lot of climbing went on in *The Tempest*. The well end of the deck was empty except for several tables and a few chairs. As they talked, the two men leaned against the railing, one leaning more heavily than the other.

"When did you get back?" Porliss asked, politely but without much interest.

"Last night. I've only got a few days before I have to be in Santa Fe. I thought it wouldn't hurt to look in on you. Is everything holding up all right?"

Brocken was referring to the costumes. He was always a little anxious about costumes once the actors got into them. He did not like actors much. In his view they were destructive, often barbarous– a necessary evil at best.

"No jet lag?"

Brocken shrugged. "No more than usual. It's a habit with me."

"You look awful. Exhausted, I mean."

"Thanks, Hobie. You certainly know how to make a bloke feel good."

"Sorry, but you should take care of yourself," Porliss insisted.

"A vacation maybe? A couple of weeks in the Caribbean? People say St. Barts is lovely. I'd love to, but I can't on the money you people pay designers, can I?"

Porliss made a sour face. "That's not my fault."

"I know it isn't. Sorry." Brocken changed the subject. "How much time do we have?"

Porliss consulted his timepiece, a great golden turnip he wore on an antique chain and carried in a vest pocket on the right side of his paunch.

"In precisely... eleven minutes the trumpets will sound," he announced. He had a way of making most of his statements into proclamations, and delivered these with a mild southern accent, although he had, in fact, been born in Michigan. The accent resulted from his being told as a young man that he resembled Truman Capote. Porliss was also given to wearing the sort of hat that had been popular in the forties. He had directed first in Chicago, and later in other American cities, none of which was New York. Nevertheless, he gained a reputation for success with what is sometimes called the "American Repertoire," which is to say, several plays by Tennessee Williams, a couple by Arthur Miller, and, on rare occasion, something by Eugene O'Neill. Porliss was first brought to Stratford to direct *Camino Real*, and had made a success of it. He returned a few years later with *A Moon for the Misbegotten*, which most people hated but for some reason the critics liked. Eventually, he became a more or less regular visiting director and sometime actor. Finally he drifted, as Tennessee might have said, into Shakespeare.

"You mean the trumpets will sound if all goes well," Brocken observed. He was nothing if not a pessimist, as are many of those who work backstage in the great theatres of the world. He even looked pessimistic, dark and dry and worn.

"What could go wrong?" Porliss said. "This isn't opening night after all. The play is running smoothly..."

"Smoothly? Even in Europe I heard that you were having trouble with Sandra."

Porliss shook his head emphatically. "Not serious trouble. She has bad nights but they don't show onstage."

"Bad nights? Don't tell me she's in love again."

"I'm afraid so."

"Another gay actor?" Brocken guessed. "Will she never learn?"

"I almost wish it were that. She'd be treated more kindly... No, it's Alan Wales, I'm afraid."

"That ass-kissing Ken doll? I don't believe it. She has better taste."

Porliss nodded solemnly. "I've talked with her about it, but she won't listen to reason."

"Lovers don't. It's not their *métier*. I hate that kid. Even by dress rehearsal he still hadn't learned to get into his baldrick properly. He makes his costume look like it ought to be in a gangster movie."

"As often as not he wears his tunic backwards, so the heraldry on his chest doesn't show."

"Is he still carrying around that pig-sticker of a knife? Dangerous damn thing to have onstage... or anywhere else for that matter."

"I tried to get him to give it up," Porliss said, "but he is so attached to it..."

"Oh, Hobie..." Brocken growled, like a bull mastiff about to bite. "I should have put him in something long and flowing– like the Avon River."

"It's his entrances that I can't stand," Porliss said. "He comes onstage as if the play were some bad film version of *A Chorus Line*. That's what he wants, of course. That's why he's here. He sees Stratford as a stepping stone to Hollywood."

"Well, if you feel like that, why did you cast him?"

Porliss shrugged. "Unfortunately I haven't always felt about Alan the way I feel now."

"Not you, too!"

"I'm afraid so, dear boy. He would never have been in the company if I hadn't persuaded Ziemski-Trapp that he had potential."

Brocken snorted. "Potential! That's an odd word for it."

"Actually it's a very precise term for it. Lots and lots of potential. But that was two seasons ago. He's gone on to others now..."

"Sandra..."

"Sandra at the very least. I don't know who else he's screwing but one was never enough. I've heard he has a girl from town."

"How can you be sure it's a girl?"

"I can't," Porliss said with a sigh. "I have reason enough, however, to believe that he prefers girls. He only does men when he's trying to get on with his profession."

"His profession! Surely you don't mean acting?"

"I did, but now that you mention it..."

Brocken thought for a moment. "Two seasons ago you say. If all that happened two seasons ago, why the hell is he in *Mac*–"

Porliss broke into Brocken's question abruptly. "Don't say it! We've problems enough as it is."

"In the Scottish Play, then. I don't understand why you're still using him."

Porliss laughed slightly, sadly. "I'm not using him, dear boy. He's using me."

"The little pig is blackmailing you?"

"Not for money, but..."

"...but he makes you cast him."

"*Voilà!*" Porliss said simply.

"Hobie, why do you let him get away with it? Everyone knows about you anyway."

Porliss drew himself up and for a moment looked almost tall, almost impressive.

"What," he demanded, "does everyone know?"

"Listen, Hobie. This is George... your old friend. I don't want to hurt your feelings, but everyone knows you're an old queen... an old queen with a great flair for theatre. As you say: *voilà!*"

Briefly, Porliss glared, then the glare passed and he slumped into his familiar pudgy form. He looked as if he were about to cry.

"I don't like being gossiped about," he said weakly.

"Well, you're sure as hell in the wrong trade, then." Brocken squinted at his friend. "The heart of the matter is, you're still hooked on the little whore."

Porliss put his plump right hand to his eyes and held it there a moment or so. When he looked again at Brocken, there was no hint of a tear.

"Yes, George," he said, "that *is* the heart of the matter. But you know, it's funny, I'd be just as happy if he were somehow out of my sight and life altogether."

Brocken shook his head, then gazed out across the cricket field toward the river and Lake Victoria. The water was dark, brightened only by the passage of a single cruising swan. The willows lining the shores trembled in an uncertain breeze. The few leaves that remained turned up their undersides.

They're like the silver bellies of dead fish, Brocken thought with the designer's side of his mind.

Looking still farther away to the south, he saw that clouds were building on the horizon. He was calmer when he spoke again, and so was Porliss.

"There'll be a storm tonight," he said.

Porliss too looked at the clouds. "Possible. We've had lots of rain this summer. I'm glad we're not playing in a tent."

"Are you? I don't know. There are fewer technical problems in a theatre, I suppose, but bad weather can add to the drama. Real thunder has a quality that canned effects can never match."

"What a romantic you are, George! Real thunder!" He chuckled, then let the chuckle grow to laughter, the grand overstated laughter of a fat actor. Porliss was a man who believed in "canned effects." Even his bad productions were often praised for their "effects."

"I brought you a present, Hobie." Brocken rummaged in the shopping bag he was carrying, a large fuchsia reticule with "Printemps-Paris" lavishly inscribed on either side of it. He always carried a shopping bag, and it was usually a bag from some distant place. Like most theatre designers, he was often in distant places.

"A present? For me?" Porliss was delighted. He loved being brought things, especially good things to eat, which is what people usually brought him; he was a notorious gourmand.

"I got it yesterday in Stuttgart," Brocken said, as he pulled a smaller bag from the larger. It was fouled in Burano lace—another gift, but for a favourite cutter, not for Porliss. Finally he liberated the small bag and held it out to the director. The bag was black and was decorated with a caricature of a face.

"Who's that?" Porliss asked. "Mozart again?"

"Goethe. I got it in a bookstore."

Porliss accepted the offering. It was heavy, much heavier than he had expected. He fumbled the black bundle, then clutched it to his belly.

"Jesus, George! This thing's heavy."

"It's cast iron," Brocken explained blandly. "Cast iron is generally rather heavy."

Porliss stripped away the black plastic and revealed a squat bust of a bearded man. The director looked puzzled.

"Thanks awfully," he said, "but why me?"

Brocken grinned wickedly. "Don't you recognize him?"

"Should I?"

"It's Shakespeare, or at least, it's some central European's version of Shakespeare. A dealer in Wittenburg is turning them out like hot cakes."

"The Hamlet connection, I suppose."

"Probably. Anyway, they're everywhere in Europe. I picked up several of them. I thought you'd be amused."

"Oh I am, dear boy. I am. It'll make a splendid... a splendid..."

"Hat stand?" Brocken supplied.

"Or maybe I could turn it upside down and use it for an ashtray..." Porliss suggested doubtfully.

The fanfare sounded on the other side of the theatre.

"Rats!" Brocken muttered. "I was going to have a drink before the ordeal."

"There's still time," Porliss said. He looked uncomfortably at his gift, then set it down on the edge of the well. He peered at the bust as if it were the solution to some great puzzle. Back in the days when he was acting more than directing, he had been known for his tendency to overplay his scenes. He leaned back, peered again. Very slowly he walked in a circle around the well, his gaze remaining on the bust of Shakespeare.

"You run along," Porliss said at last. "I'll stay here a moment longer to contemplate the beauty of this... thing."

Brocken exited toward the bar, laughing unpleasantly, which was his way of laughing.

(2:2) The dressing room of Seamus O'Reilly

Seamus O'Reilly was getting into character. He was already in full make-up, including the shaggy, overbeetling eyebrows and bristling beard he had been given for his portrayal of Duncan. He already had the complexion for the part, the weathered forehead and cheeks, the purplish bloom on the nose.

He was also in costume, or in most of it. He delayed putting on the great fur cloak he was obliged to wear in his early scenes. O'Reilly loved the cloak, treated it with the affection that most men would reserve for a favourite dog, but it was too hot for the dressing room. It was too hot for the stage as well, but out there heat didn't matter. Nothing mattered then but the play, or rather, nothing mattered but the performance, his performance, which wasn't always in perfect agreement with the play.

Even in his ordinary clothes– not that he had any *ordinary* clothes– O'Reilly had the knack of making himself look many of the parts that Shakespeare had written for mature players.

"Shakespeare must have known a lot of old actors," O'Reilly had been heard to say more than once, "and he must have liked them better than he liked old actresses."

But character... that was a serious matter.

He ran over his opening lines, rumbling through them rapidly to set them even more firmly in his memory.

"What bloody man is that..." he mumbled, rushing along without interpretation or volume, merely to set the lines more firmly in his mind, a "spaghetti run" as the method was sometimes known.

O'Reilly had trouble with his lines nowadays. He rarely left a line out, and he never lost the metre. He did, however, have a tendency to jumble phrases, to put them in the wrong order. This trifling fault, as he thought of it, bothered his colleagues more than it did him, as it frequently confounded their cues and brought them into a scene where they didn't belong and where they weren't wanted.

"Every word was there," O'Reilly would boom when challenged on this matter. "Every blessed word."

Part of his pre-performance routine was to make faces—"working the phiz," he called it.

He was leering hideously in the middle of these facial gymnastics when the door to his dressing room opened behind him. A head was thrust round the edge of the doorway, the exquisite head of Alan Wales. Wales never bothered to get into any character other than his own. Nor did he dress or make up until the very last minute.

"Break a leg, Seamus," Wales said. "I mean that."

O'Reilly whirled in his chair and grabbed at something to throw.

"Bugger off!" he thundered, and a projectile flashed across the little room. It was a full pound jar of cleansing cream which had been launched with both power and accuracy from O'Reilly's mighty arm. It struck the door post. The impact shattered the heavy jar, and it would have shattered the face of Alan Wales, had that face not vanished in the nick of time.

(2:3) The dressing room of Alessandra Edel

Sandra's dressing room was as chaotic as her borrowed apartment. There were boxes and bags and indiscriminate heaps everywhere. Her dressing table was a No Man's Land of weird bottles, tubes, and packets. Her wardrobe stood open and spilled its rainbow-coloured guts into the room. All the drawers in her bureau yawned gaudily; on top was a jumble of purses, sunglasses, handkerchiefs, lipsticks, small change and other money– dollars of two nations, francs of two more, pounds, lire, marks and pesos.

Sandra was studying herself in the mirror above the dressing table. Heavy with the regalia of queenliness, weighed down by barbaric jewels, she was as elaborately and artificially beautiful as a saint in a Byzantine painting.

"It's the eyes," she said sombrely to the image in the mirror. "It's the eyes that always go first."

She raised a slightly trembling hand and with her finger-tips adjusted the crow's wing of fake eyelash that hovered over the iris of her right eye. "The poor eyes..."

There was a knock at her dressing room door.

"*Entrez*," she said without looking away from the mirror. When she saw who it was who had entered, however, she rose immediately and turned to meet him.

"Alan!" she said. The smile on her richly painted face was large enough to endanger her entire brittle façade. Her smile gleamed for a moment, then vanished as quickly as it had come. "But you aren't dressed yet."

"I'm on my way now," Wales said, sweeping his dark hair away from his brow with a long-fingered hand, "but I couldn't go past your door without looking in."

Sandra was pleased. "You are naughty."

Wales approached her, his eyes heavy with sultry invitation. His lips parted to make a small smile, the smile of a lustful faun. He tried the smile on everyone he met.

"Don't even think about it, darling," Sandra said, still with undisguised pleasure. "I'll smudge."

Wales moved even closer and put his hand inside the heavily boned and wired confection that supported Sandra's queenly bosom.

"No, Alan," she sighed, "please... you must go get dressed."

Wales withdrew the hand roughly.

"What a bore you are sometimes," he snarled.

"Please, darling..."

"I know, I know. Get dressed," Wales said petulantly. "I hate my stupid costume."

"Don't be angry," Sandra said anxiously, as if she were already far too aware of what Alan Wales was like when angry. "Come round to my place after the show. We'll have a glass of wine and there'll be no rush. But not now, darling. There's no time..."

Wales pouted.

"Please..."

"All right, Sandra, I'm on my way."

"Come to me tonight."

"Maybe, I don't know," Wales mumbled.

He moved toward the door, then stopped again. "Can you lend me a quarter? I forgot to call Maury about that audition."

"You can't call now. There's no time."

"Will you lend me the quarter or not?"

"Of course, but..." She gestured toward the chest-of-drawers.

Wales rummaged quickly through the litter on top of the bureau until he found the coin he required.

"Thanks," he said briefly on his way out.

"Will I see you... later...?"

"Maybe," he called over his shoulder as he shut the door behind him. Out in the corridor he pocketed the quarter. He also pocketed the twenty dollar bill he had palmed while hunting for the coin.

(2:4) A corridor

Wales was whistling as he swaggered down the corridor. He did not see Grace Lockhardt squeezed in a corner near Sandra's dressing room. She was bringing a small silver necklace to Sandra, a part of Lady Macbeth's costume which had mysteriously migrated across the theatre underworld to someone else's dressing room.

It was not surprising that Grace was invisible to Alan Wales; she did not have the sort of looks he would condescend to notice (nor any important connections to make up for her absence of glamour). To him, her face was too bony, her nose overly pointed, her marble pallor unforgivable in this age of tanning salons. Grace's eyes were an ordinary brown with perhaps a bit too much warmth in them, and her thin lips at the moment were pressed so tightly together that they seemed no more than a line hastily drawn by a hurried artist.

And certainly, Wales would have had no patience whatsoever with the barely perceptible rise of her breasts, or with legs which, while uncommonly shapely, were far too short for the uses to which Alan Wales liked to put legs.

Grace twisted the small necklace in her tiny, fragile hands as she struggled to hold back tears while muttering to herself:

"Why do you let yourself be treated that way? You're too wonderful, too beautiful for him... he doesn't know you, he doesn't appreciate you... Sandra– he doesn't love you..."

She said something else to herself about love, but not aloud; she whispered it deep inside her soul, where no one but she would ever hear. Then she wiped her eyes with the back of her hand and took a deep and steadying breath before going in to complete her mistress' perfection.

(2:5) By a window

Keyes had managed to wangle his way backstage to extend handshakes, good wishes, and even kisses to those company members and crew with whom he had kept in contact over the years. He had a slight twinge of nostalgia for the hurly-burly of his former profession, but this passed quickly. It was much less stressful and much more fun to be audience, especially with his insider's knowledge of how it all worked. For Keyes the magic had never been spoiled or damaged by his intimate understanding of how lights and trapdoors and set-painting contributed to the transformation of the mundane into the marvellous.

As a harried assistant stage manager shooed him out to join the rest of the paying customers, Keyes heard her mumble, "Where the hell is Wales...?" before she went rushing off to don her headset, to become, in essence, Second Master of the Revels.

Keyes decided he had just enough time for a brief cigarette before curtain time, and finally found an area marked SMOKING where there was also a window for him to gaze out of.

He saw a curious thing.

Just outside of the rear of the theatre, near one of the several bolt-hole doors provided for actors like O'Reilly to escape their adoring public, he saw Alan Wales, in full costume, in what looked like earnest conversation with someone. The girl seemed quite exotic. She looked very young, with waist-length black hair of a hue that lent itself to purple highlights in the right circumstances, and an impressive shapeliness not suggested but stated outright by a short red dress that also said "go to hell," and spike-heeled shoes that supplied directions. The dress was covered in sequins which added a dash of déclassé glamour to the dim dusk outside.

Although Keyes could hear nothing of their conversation, the gestures the couple used indicated a disagreement of some kind; for a moment, Keyes thought the girl was about to strike Wales across his handsome face, but then her hand dropped to her side, fiddling nervously with what there was of her hemline. Wales suddenly grabbed her, pulled her to him, and kissed her with what Keyes thought was cold and careless brutality. Then Wales turned his back on her, and disappeared inside the theatre.

The girl stared after Wales for a moment, then she too turned and strode away, with a calculated walk that made Keyes feel underage.

The fanfare sounded, as if ending the tableau. Keyes extinguished his cigarette and found his way to his seat, eager to immerse himself in the blood and madness of the first act of the Scottish Play.

(2:6) The Festival Theatre, grounds

Now the environs of the Festival Theatre became oddly desolate. Only moments before the lawns and gardens, the sidewalks and streets round about, had teemed with people. Gossiping aimlessly, laughing, flirting and boasting, they strolled here and there waiting for the play to start, or more precisely, waiting for the fanfare to sound. When it did, when the trumpets began to bray and blast, the crowd was suddenly transformed. The people in the throng lost their individuality and moved as one. Every head turned toward the entrance to the great house; every foot edged or hopped or shuffled in that direction. Like autumn leaves caught in a flash flood, the audience swirled about, then quickly disappeared into the theatre, as if down a mighty drain, leaving no one outside—no one at all.

There were, of course, relics of this multitude that had so abruptly vanished. Paper cups and cigarette butts had been tossed too carelessly at the containers provided for them. A newspaper had been dropped, and a text of the Scottish Play, and a lace handkerchief. Someone had left an umbrella leaning against a concrete pillar. Someone else had forgotten a straw hat on a retaining wall.

Hobart Porliss had forgotten, or pretended to forget, the bust of Shakespeare which he had just acquired from George Brocken. It balanced unsteadily where he had left it, staring across the yawn of the well-hole.

Like the abandoned umbrella and the straw hat, this squat iron effigy of the Bard, which had been made to seem almost barbarous by the clumsiness, or perhaps the Expressionismus, of its distant creator, was entirely impervious to the trumpets' blast. Not even with a glance did it acknowledge the entertainment that the horns had announced. Instead, the black iron eyes concentrated on something in the distance, something far beyond the terrace, beyond the deserted cricket field. The eyes stared at the river and at a drifting swan— a thing of grace, of delicacy, and of impeccable whiteness.

At eight o'clock, the traditional cannon was discharged to signal the beginning of the evening's performance; the echoing boom set the deck to vibrating for a moment. The bust wobbled on the lip of the well, then tumbled with a loud, hollow ring to the pavement below.

(2:7) The Festival Theatre, intermission

Keyes waited for the intermission in *Macbeth* with an anticipation he usually reserved for sex or fine liquor; despite Sandra's assurance that "Porliss knows what he's doing," it was Keyes' opinion that Porliss did *not* know what he was doing, not quite.

Porliss had managed, however, to use to the fullest the excellence of most of his actors. Damian Pace's Macbeth was sound, and certainly Seamus O'Reilly knew what he was about. If anything, O'Reilly's Duncan was too strong; it threatened to overshadow the title role even with many fewer lines and scenes. Sandra's Lady Macbeth was fine, rich and complicated. The rest of the actors were performing with the solid competence for which the company was so well known.

What, then? Keyes asked himself. What's wrong with the thing?

For a while he was convinced it was the set. George Brocken's designs were commendable– indeed they drew applause from the audience when the lights first went up– but they did not wear well. With his wrought iron structures and the stark shadow patterns that they cast across the stage, Brocken was trying to represent primitive architectural forms, but also to suggest cages, the traps that were slowly closing around the Thane of Glamis and Cawdor. But by the time Duncan was murdered, and O'Reilly removed from the play, the once-elegant décors were beginning to remind Keyes of scrap iron and junkyards, which was not, he suspected, the artist's intention.

"Less would have been more," Keyes muttered, which caused the serious young school teacher sitting beside him to glare and put her finger to her mouth.

Hobart Porliss' penchant for special effects and elaborate make-up was also getting in the way. Keyes came to the theatre for Shakespeare's language more than anything else. So far as he was concerned, anything that got in the way of the poetry was a mistake, almost a criminal mistake. Here there were many such errors; important blocks of text were missing or relocated, and lines were spoken that Keyes was certain he had never heard or read before.

Both O'Reilly and Sandra had excellent diction and superb control of their voices, and in their scenes the poetry (or what remained of it after Porliss' editing) not only survived, it soared. In other scenes, however, the lines were too mired in gore to have much meaning. Watching these scenes Keyes found himself wondering about the harried crew member whose job it was to apply stage-blood to the cast.

"Must be spraying it on with a garden-hose," he grumbled.

"Shh!" hissed the teacher.

"Sorry," Keyes apologized. As he did, he looked at the woman carefully for the first time. He had noticed her pretty mouth earlier. Now he saw that the rest of her was pretty. She was pretty enough to make him feel sorry that he had disturbed her concentration on the play.

He slumped into his seat and closed his eyes.

"O horror, horror, horror..." someone bellowed from the far side of the stage.

Strangely, the words took Keyes entirely away from the play and out of the theatre. "Horror" made him remember another scene, the one he had witnessed between Alan Wales and his girlfriend. Something about it had been truly horrible, and more fraught with terrible possibility than what he had paid forty dollars to watch on the stage.

When the intermission came (in a totally inappropriate place, probably arranged so that the stage could be mopped), Keyes was still thinking about Wales and his friend. Instead of rushing to the bar as he usually did at interval time, he went outside. The storm that had threatened all day had come and gone during the early scenes of the play. Large puddles of rainwater stood on the pavement in front of the theatre. The flowers in their concrete planters leaned groggily this way and that after the beating they had taken from the downpour. The lawns were sodden.

Keyes lit a cigarette, and wandered, not quite aimlessly, toward the river side of the theatre. He reached the Marquee deck near the well-hole where George Brocken and Hobart Porliss had recently discussed storms. Then, continuing his long flirtation with lung cancer, he lit another cigarette, leaning slightly over the well to shield flame from wind.

For a moment the flare of his cigarette lighter blinded him. As his eyes were recovering, he saw a sharp, intense flicker of some other light from below. Perhaps because he had spent part of the evening watching witches, he sensed something infernal in the light, something wickedly faerie.

"Too late in the year for fireflies," he said to no one in particular, or perhaps to the after-image of the flicker itself, commanding it to explain its presence.

He squinted down into the shadows. The light from the theatre's shop windows was dim and bled on the scene from an angle, but Keyes could see something huddled on the ground. It was vaguely manlike, a sprawling form. Someone must have slipped on the wet grass, or perhaps even fallen through the well-hole, Keyes supposed. He squinted again, then headed for the stairs to see if he could help whoever it was.

A moment later he stood looking down on the prone figure of one of Macbeth's bleeding sergeants.

Keyes shook his head in amused disgust: Alan Wales seemed to be imitating certain eccentricities of Seamus O'Reilly, whom Keyes had once come upon dead drunk and passed out in full costume, much like this; except, to O'Reilly's credit, the curtain had already come down for the evening.

Besides Wales' head, inexplicably, was another head: that of William Shakespeare, cast in iron. Keyes bent down to give Wales a shake, only to be shaken himself when he realized that the thick liquid leaking onto his hand from the corner of the actor's mouth was warm– it was not part of the bloody man's stage make-up, but real blood. Keyes quickly placed his fingers against Wales' neck. There was no pulse.

Jean-Claude Keyes had died the thousand deaths on the boards, had read the daily deaths in the newspapers, had seen slow-motion deaths on screen, but this was his first encounter with the real thing. Turning aside, he lost his breakfast, lunch, dinner, and what little naïveté remained in his heart. As Keyes raised his head, he saw the shining again, the brief glow which had brought him here, just off to his left; there, in a slight indentation in the soggy earth, was a tiny pile of silvery fragments. In a daze, he picked them up and stared at them long to enough to identify them as sequins, then forgot them as he automatically reached into his pocket for his cigarettes. The star-shaped flakes drifted down the lining of his jacket to join his house keys, the stub of his ticket, and some errant lint.

Breathing deeply several times to regain his self-control, Keyes stood up. For a moment he was unable to take his eyes from the body. Alan Wales, he thought, had certainly picked an uncomfortable position in which to die. Limbs were protruding every which way. Still, there was something oddly theatrical about Wales' pose, not that it mattered to him now that his acting was ended permanently.

"He wasn't this dramatic onstage tonight," Keyes said softly. Then, he heard a voice above him and cocked an ear in its direction, as if he was a troll at the bottom of a well listening to the song of an innocent peasant about to draw water.

(2:8) The Festival Theatre, grounds

Keyes recognized the affected drawl of Hobart Porliss.

"Where is the damned thing?" Porliss was muttering, and Keyes assumed the director was alone, since there were no other voices or footsteps. A few seconds later, Porliss' voice was followed by Porliss' face, which became puzzled as soon as he looked down and saw Keyes through the round frame of the well.

"Porliss," Keyes said without prologue, "you've got a problem."

"Only one?" Porliss asked sourly, his eyes darting about as if seeking someone other than Keyes. Then Porliss saw the body.

"This one's enough." Keyes gestured for Porliss to descend, and the fat man obliged.

He stared at the corpse.

"Alan...?"

Keyes nodded.

"Is he...? I mean he looks..."

"He is," Keyes said.

"Alan..." Porliss murmured again, with an intonation and expression Keyes could not quite interpret; it seemed almost like relief.

Porliss shook his head, as if to clear it. "This is terrible—he's got the Third Murderer to do yet!" Then, as if realizing how he must sound, Porliss hurriedly went on: "I mean, how awful... the poor boy..."

"Somebody has to call the police," Keyes said.

"Right now? Couldn't we wait until the play is over?" Porliss suggested.

"Hobie, this is serious, not a bad dress rehearsal!"

"Alan had enough of those," Porliss said, almost smiling this time, Keyes thought. "But you're right. God, this could ruin me, absolutely *ruin* me!"

Keyes refrained from saying that Porliss' ruin as a director was a *fait accompli*, and by his own hand at that. Then a monumental shadow fell over them, and a voice boomed in their ears.

"What's going on down there?" Porliss and Keyes craned their necks around and up to see O'Reilly peering over the rim. He, too, was covered in gore, the blood spilt at Duncan's murder. Unlike the blood on Alan Wales, however, none of his was real. "Never mind, I'll come see for myself!" His head disappeared from the opening.

Dressed as he was in the regalia of the Dark Ages, it was not easy for O'Reilly to negotiate ramp and stair down to the alcove beneath the well. The great cloak of wolf pelts caught on the webbing of ropes and ladders.

When O'Reilly arrived, in a swirl of fur and leather, Porliss still stood staring at the dead man. Keyes turned to meet O'Reilly.

"It's Wales," Keyes said; then added, diplomatically, "he's had an accident."

"What do you mean, 'accident'?"

He stopped, and like Porliss, stared.

"Jesu!" he said in a soft voice. Not even as Othello in his tenderest love scene, Keyes thought, had O'Reilly spoken so softly, so gently.

O'Reilly had to bend down to see clearly what had happened to Wales, the lighting being so feeble, and the scene further obscured by the barred shadows from the rigging. Nevertheless O'Reilly instantly knew that Wales was dead. He put forward a hand, thought better of what he was doing, and straightened again. Then he noticed the iron bust, and pointed to it.

"Who's that?"

"Shakespeare," explained Keyes.

"What the hell's it doing here... although Will would have loved this!"

"It's mine..." Porliss said in a vague fashion. "I left it up there... on the rim of the well..."

"But what happened?" O'Reilly demanded. He glanced upward. "Did Wales fall through that ridiculous hole? It's not a very long drop..."

"I don't know," Keyes said, "but the blood on his face is real, and a couple of his teeth are broken– maybe somebody hit him with something."

"There are plenty of people around with reason to... to hit him, as you say. I've wanted to hit him myself..."

"But not that hard," Keyes suggested.

O'Reilly shook his ponderous head slowly. "No, not that hard." Then the big actor shook his head again, more briskly, as if clearing it for more important concerns. "Hobart– what about the Third Murderer?"

The show must go on, Keyes thought. What madmen actors were...

"There are only a few lines..." Porliss replied. "I'll do it myself."

"You won't be able to get into his costume– *he* barely squeezed into it!" O'Reilly said sardonically.

Porliss shuddered so violently that Keyes thought for a moment he might shake himself to pieces.

"Take it easy, Hobie," Keyes said. Although he didn't care for Porliss, neither did he like to see so much distress in him. He didn't like seeing it in anyone. Keyes put his hand on the plump shoulder in an effort to steady Porliss, or console him, or something. The trembling stopped.

"I'll wear something of yours, Seamus," Porliss said, and drew himself up in an effort to look as if he were in command– of himself, if not of the situation.

"We'd better call the police," Keyes insisted.

"It must have been an accident," Porliss put in frantically. "Right now, we've got a show to finish!"

"Duncan's dead," O'Reilly said. "*You've* got a show to finish. *I'm* going to get drunk."

Porliss rolled his eyes, then said, more or less to himself, "George... George will find something for me to wear."

"You're still worrying about the Third Murderer?" O'Reilly growled. "Play the scene with two murderers."

"There are three murderers in the text," Porliss proclaimed. "There is the integrity of the text to think about."

O'Reilly snorted, "In this production? You've already butchered the text. One more cut won't even be noticed. *I* think Shakespeare threw that part in at the last minute for some friend of his, anyway. Nobody will know, Hobart."

"I will know," Porliss said in pious tones. "And God will know."

"Give me a break," O'Reilly moaned, as he surveyed the body again. "You know, I believe he's wearing his costume correctly at last, so some good has come out of it. He's even managed to strike a decent pose. Looks a bit like a hieroglyph, doesn't he?"

Keyes was having trouble believing his ears. A man lay dead between them, and these two lunatics were talking about cut lines and costuming!

"The police!" he repeated. "Somebody has to do something about... this." He gestured vaguely toward the corpse, then as if possessed by some long-buried swashbuckling instinct, Keyes began to clamber up a rope-ladder which dangled from the lip of the well. Once, this would have been an efficient decision, allowing him to reach the Marquee deck more quickly. But, given the intervening years of physical inactivity, he made rather heavy weather of the ascent, and nearly fell, which could easily have resulted in his lying sprawled senseless beside Alan Wales.

"See if you can find George Brocken for me," Porliss called.

When Keyes reached the nearest door, he found his way blocked by a small, birdlike woman.

"Is Mr. Porliss out there?" Grace Lockhardt asked. "It's almost time to go again."

"Yes, he's down below... but you stay here. Have you seen George Brocken?"

Grace shook her head. "Not backstage. He's in the house, somebody said."

Keyes glanced past the dresser and saw Sandra coming down a flight of stairs. She was wearing a nightdress smeared with blood. What has happened to company discipline? Keyes thought with somewhat tangential censure. What kind of show had half its cast running around outside at intermission, covered with false blood?

Sandra called to them uncertainly. "For God's sake, Grace, what are you doing out there? I need you."

"Get her out of here," Keyes whispered to Grace.

"But what about Mr. Porliss?"

"He'll be along. Please, go!"

She went as she was told and intercepted Sandra on the stairs. The two women spoke briefly in hushed tones, then Sandra looked across at Keyes.

"Claude?" she said. "What is it?"

Keyes shook his head, and directed her back upstairs with a wave of his hand.

"Nothing," he lied. "A little accident. There's no time now. I'll talk to you later."

"Later?" Sandra echoed. "Later?"

Somewhere above her, places were called. Her eyes widened, then she turned away to climb toward the stage and the appalling challenge of her role as Lady Macbeth.

(2:9) A street

Keyes managed to contact the police; they arrived after the play had resumed, and were initially able to question only those not onstage, primarily Keyes. He answered methodically, to the best of his ability, and escaped just as the first members of the audience emerged through the front doors of the theatre.

Keyes walked slowly back to Betty's; he wanted to change his clothes, have a quiet drink, and think about this sudden and grisly event for a while before he was forced into the inevitable post mortems. The night was unseasonably warm, pleasant now that the storm had passed, and the air smelled fresh, as if it had been washed free of any unpleasantness, cleansed even of blood. This neighbourhood, adjacent to the Festival, was quietly residential, with well-kept homes and carefully ordered gardens. Trees in bright seasonal costume lined the sidewalk; they bowed gently in the autumn wind, nodding sagely to Keyes, as he eavesdropped on a couple across the street loudly analyzing the shortcomings of *Macbeth*.

"I've never *seen* so much blood in one play!" said the man, brushing a stray leaf from his tuxedo jacket. "Really, I don't see the artistic necessity in splattering every second person with a gallon of red paint!"

The heavy and heavily-gowned woman hanging from his arm answered in a confrontational New York voice, "Oh, but I don't agree, Justin! It's all allegorical, you know, the director's symbolic commentary on how messy political ambition is. *I* thought it was absolutely *brilliant*. The *real* horror in that show was those *wigs*. Just *awful*..."

"Oh, I agree," the man continued, "but you know what was really interesting? How much better the second half was, after the intermission. Somebody or other must have given a rousing pep-talk..."

"Or made dire threats!" the woman laughed.

Keyes stopped listening, and wondered what symbolic meaning these armchair critics would attach to the bloodied corpse of Alan Wales.

From the notebook of Jean-Claude Keyes:

Literature. Painting. Theatre– does anyone really care if sometimes the seams show, or that the collar occasionally doesn't match the cuffs? In the middle of an economic depression (not so named, but everyone knows the monster for what it is), wars, famine, ozone depletion, does it matter if a band of painted players does or does not get the words in the right order and manages not to bump into the furniture?

Yes, I say, it does matter– to people like Seamus, and Sandra... and to me; and yet, for the life of me, I'm still not quite sure why... I think it has something to do with how we use art as a tool to deal with the above-mentioned chaos and horror of everyday existence in the modern world, how music and plays and films give shape and form to our own insignificant dramas, thereby allowing us to understand ourselves just a bit more clearly. Even the primary-colour slapstick of Saturday morning cartoons sometimes has the power to make us smile and see our trials and tribulations as not quite so insurmountable, and if such trivialities as these can ever so slightly reshape the world, how much more might be accomplished by a bravura performance of one of Shakespeare's little entertainments, charged as they are with the best and the worst in the human spirit?

It strikes me that if these notes were to be reviewed, the notice would certainly be a bad one– I sound like budget Beckett. Must be death that's put me in such a mood.

Laurence Olivier had giant talent, but he is dead; Alan Wales had (as far as I could tell) no talent, and he is dead, too. Death is the cruellest but most fair of all critics. One bad write-up from Death, and your career is really finished, but at least Death plays no favourites, takes no bribes, prints no retractions (not that mortal critics do, either!), and in the end, most certainly is not proud.

ACT THREE

Babbling Gossip of the Air

For murder, though it have no tongue, will speak
With most miraculous organ...
– *Hamlet,* Act II, Scene 2

(3:1) Betty's Bed & Breakfast

Later, at Betty's, the conversation was of Wales' death. While Betty Beardsley was not technically of Stratford's theatrical community, she kept in touch with it, went to openings, attended all the parties, and was acquainted with most of the people.

"Did you know him?" Keyes asked. Betty's face warped into an expression more suited to the contemplation of garbage, reminding Keyes of the contempt in which O'Reilly had held Wales, when Wales was alive.

"He lived here briefly, when I was naïve enough to think it would be nice to have actors in the house; I would have been better off to open a hostel for alcoholics and drug addicts! I may yet– there are all sorts of government grants for that sort of thing..."

"Not a model tenant, then?"

"He used my eighteenth century china saucers for ash-trays!" she said, as if that explained everything; when she saw how unimpressed Keyes was by the perfidy of this particular sin, she went on: "He had people over partying after every show, till three and four o'clock in the morning. I found ashes in the carpet and beer bottles in the umbrella stand... and once, when I returned from Toronto after an audition, I found a naked ingenue in *my* bed. I think he stole a couple of fairly valuable items from me, too, but I couldn't prove it. When I threw him out, I told him he was lucky I didn't kill him. I hate thieves, and I hate finding nude women in my bed– you never know where they've been! And as an actor, well– if *he's* an *actor*, then *I'm* an orangutan's Great Aunt Elvira! Far be it from me to be vindictive, but I can't help thinking the world is no poorer without Wales; he was a self-centred, unprincipled, scheming, lying– "

Keyes cut her off before she really got going.

"If you didn't like him, Betty, why not just come right out and say it without all this beating around the bush?"

"Very funny. But it wasn't just the way he treated me. He used everybody badly, once he had charmed them into being off-guard– he was *very* good at that. His affair with Sandra Edel..." Betty shook her head with great and sincere sympathy.

Keyes nodded in agreement. "Sandra has always required a great deal of affection, or at least the show of affection. And she's very stubborn about trying to keep what she has."

"Aren't we all," Betty agreed.

"Some more than others," Keyes said, rising from the table. "Maybe O'Reilly's right and theatre is all about love. Seamus mentioned to me that a lot of people disliked this boy. I wouldn't want to be a cop investigating this. Sounds to me like sorting out motive alone will be complicated and unpleasant. And who knows? Maybe it *was* just an accident, after all. I suppose it's none of my business, anyway. I gave *my* statement, and I for one have no motive at all. Good night, Betty."

Wearily, Keyes traversed the hallway to his lonely bed. He stopped for a moment to admire again his favourite original Betty Beardsley painting. He liked the enthusiastic style, the bold brush-strokes. The subject was a wedding dinner; thirteen figures, who looked Mediterranean, were positioned around the table in the poses of da Vinci's "The Last Supper." The bride's expression was anything but a happy one, and it was Keyes' private opinion that the man in the picture who occupied the Judas position was the groom.

Keyes' thoughts held none of the cool disdain which he had displayed for Betty's benefit. That had been an attitude, a mask to hide how much the death had disturbed him. If Wales had mistreated Sandra, he was certainly no friend of Claude Keyes', even posthumously. Had he known of any mistreatment of Sandra prior to this night, Keyes might conceivably have found himself bound by duty and old love to seek out Mr. Wales and punch him in the nose. Therefore, he did have a motive of sorts; and he was uncertain as to how he felt about this stranger's demise. What he wanted to feel was nothing. To forget about the event and be at peace.

He was denied this by his dreams.

Three creatures populated a dreamscape of stark simplicity; a plain of stunted and warped trees stretched far off into the distance, a place of darkness broken only by the occasional flash of what might have been light. The beings, while very different, were all Claude Keyes.

One was very young, perhaps ten years old, a boy with woman's breasts who stood weeping over an indistinct pile which suddenly became the corpse of a dog, a cat, a fish, a turtle...

Nearby was Keyes again, but a grown Keyes of cold metal, an automaton of gears and switches, performing an incomprehensible set of actions over and over again, but each time executing one manoeuvre or other with some small alteration, as if attempting to find the correct method amid an infinity of choices...

And the last, seated like Zeus on a marble throne, cold and dispassionate, analyzing and judging all events and persons (and especially his other selves), and somewhat titillated– as gods are– by the majestic sweeping presence of death in its icy glory...

It was a very long and unpleasant night.

(3:2) A bookshop

Keyes woke very late the next morning to the pit-pat of more rain on the roof, and thought of the pub, but unthought it very quickly; O'Reilly would surely be there, not having any shows today, and, as close as they were, Keyes simply wasn't up to him. There would be uproar and confusion everywhere else in the insular world of the Stratford theatre community, and he wished to put off involvement with the aftermath of the death as long as possible. A bookshop, that's what was needed, an hour's browsing, maybe even a purchase or two to cure the dismal blues he had awakened with. Stratford boasted several good booksellers, including the Festival Bookshop itself, and New Land Books, which prided itself on carrying an eclectic range of literature, non-fiction, and Canadian publications. There was also a new one which Keyes hadn't yet had the opportunity to investigate.

The Book Bin turned out to be a clean and bright store on Ontario Street, with a wide selection of offbeat titles, as well as several bins of comic books, pop paraphernalia, and collector's bric-à-brac.

Keyes spent forty minutes or so thumbing through books on the history of the theatre and biographies of theatrical heavyweights, then felt someone watching him. He glanced around, and saw that he was indeed being stared at, by a young woman also browsing the costume section. He felt that he should know her from somewhere. She was very pale and slim, and wispy around the edges. Undistinguished russet hair was caught up in an unravelling bun, and she had the big, unblinking eyes of a marmoset or some such abominably cute mammal. Keyes thought that her own costuming could use an upgrade: she wore a rough ochre cotton tunic over pink and blue striped leggings, which were tucked poorly into workboots, and a bulky vest woven in colours Keyes was not even sure he had ever seen before. Sliding off one side of her head was a bright yellow beret. For some reason, her apparel seemed familiar to him, then he realized that it was a poor copy of outfits which he had seen Sandra Edel wear when she was being glamorously *outré*. The woman did not shrink under his scrutiny, merely intensified her own.

"Can I help you, miss?" he said at last, as if he were a clerk.

"You're Mr. Keyes, aren't you? Claude Keyes... Sandra's friend? We met last night briefly?"

Then he remembered: this was the young woman who had come searching for Hobart Porliss on the patio.

"Of course," he replied, bowing slightly from the waist, in keeping with her slightly askew formality.

"My name is Grace Lockhardt..."

"Oh, yes, Sandra's mentioned you. She says you're indispensable."

She flushed slightly, and seemed at a loss for words, but not for long.

"Mr. Keyes, Sandra needs us, all of her friends... now that *he's* gone; he treated her so badly and she never saw it, but now there's a chance that everybody who... who cares about her can make her see how blind she's been. It musn't happen to her again– she's too fine a person to waste herself over and over again on men who mistreat her or don't understand her–" She stopped suddenly, and flushed more deeply. "I didn't mean you, of course!"

"I understand," Keyes said. "You *are* talking about the late Mr. Wales?"

Keyes saw an expression derange Grace Lockhardt's face which he was becoming increasingly accustomed to; it was a cruel tightening of the facial muscles which said that Alan Wales being slowly roasted over a fire with split-bamboo slivers shoved under his fingernails would have been a fine sight indeed; that his death was an occasion for dancing and singing; that with his passing a small sun had returned to many people's darkened worlds.

"I'm glad he's dead!" Grace said, vehemently affirming the obvious. "Maybe now Sandra will have a chance to find real love. Please, Mr. Keyes, be her friend again. I have to go now. I'm sorry if I've bothered you."

Keyes shook his head slowly as Grace Lockhardt left the store; even her slight swaying walk resembled a distorted mirror-image of Sandra's. "*Now Sandra will have a chance to find real love...*"

And who will that love be with, in your secret dreams, Grace? Keyes thought. He continued browsing distractedly through books, wondering if perhaps one of them contained answers to such questions, or even some small hint of elusive truth.

After another fifteen minutes, Keyes could find no such truth, nor anything to hold his interest, no hefty volume in which he would be able to hide temporarily. This mental state of his was serious indeed, he told himself, when the healing power of books was ineffective. But Keyes couldn't spend much more time in this hazy half-world of questions and doubts, especially doubts which refused to be articulated– it was the current foggy quality of his thoughts which he resented most of all.

The bookshop had failed; stronger measures were obviously required.

(3:3) The Gilded Lily, a strip-joint

Keyes believed himself to be, at heart, a simple man, and believed the world itself was simple at its core– only the surface was complex and gaudy, and the simplest thing was often the most sublime. Following this philosophy, he decided to treat his glooming with a loaf of bread, a jug of wine, and by cowering in a dark corner where his regular compatriots would never stumble upon him.

"Now I'll away," he whispered as he walked along, unsure if he was remembering lines from last night's *Macbeth* or not, it having been such an unusual performance in so many ways.

Withdraw my countenance and consciousness,
Like unto–

Like unto what? Something about toads? No, that was *As You Like It*... turtles? Yes, that was it, turtles.

Like unto the crafty tortoise, pulling
Self into his armorèd Self,
There to await less mortal hours...

A hundred yards ahead along the sidewalk he spotted the place he'd chosen to wait for said safer hours, a dingy bar largely unfrequented by Festival types unless they were slumming, but that he knew from accidental experience served up a great T-bone along with the entertainment of "exotic" dancers. It was the kind of bar where too few people drank too much booze, where just enough happened to keep it in business but not enough to make the owner wealthy. It did not intimidate or threaten, nor did it plead or pimp; it simply occupied space and moved through time, and occasionally was a nondescript painted backdrop for those one-act dramas which no one would remember or record, or even remotely care about; it was not a good place or a bad place– it was just a place, where steel and dreams went to rust, and where once in a while a lonely and confused man might even glimpse a flash of newer metal, or of the Islands of the Blessed.

He left behind the misty dolour of a Stratford fall day for the smoky funk of The Gilded Lily Bar & Grill. Through a grimy window looking out onto the parking lot, Keyes saw a boom-crane For Hire truck parked outside, with the motto WE GET IT UP FOR YOU emblazoned in poor calligraphy on the door. "That just about says it all," Keyes said quietly.

He skirted the pool table inside the door, where a tall young man with a great deal of hair and very little grace scratched on a shot, cursing the ball loudly while his equally hairy girlfriend laughed hoarsely around the cigarette planted in the gap left by a missing front tooth. Keyes stopped at the bar to order his steak and a bottle of beer, then threaded his way among closely packed tables to the back corner. He passed the stage, a twelve-foot square platform of rectangular panels which flashed on and off in various neon pastels, and was raised about three feet from the floor. Around it ran a shelf or counter, and a dozen stools. Several men sat here, eating their lunch, waiting for the next entertainment to sidle through the door in the back wall.

Keyes found a small table away from the other patrons, and sat facing away from the stage– the girls were not why he was here, and he usually found their poor imitations of burlesque dancing uninteresting, anyway, even anti-erotic. There was a beer-stained copy of *The Stratford Weekly News* stuck to the tabletop. A headline screamed in larger type than he could ever recall this particular paper utilizing:

FESTIVAL ACTOR MURDERED

So, he thought, they've decided, and murder it is. He scanned the article while waiting for his meal, but there was nothing in it he didn't already know, more or less. Not even the cause of death was revealed; this information was being withheld pending further investigation. Someone of indeterminate sex arrived with his steak, and he set to eating while reading an article concerning disappearing frog populations. Below it, Keyes read this:

Swan Found Dead in Avon

Parks Board members reported finding the body of a swan floating off Tom Patterson Island early this morning. It had sustained a blow to its head, and the Swankeeper is of the opinion that it was knocked unconscious by the beak of another swan in a territorial dispute, and subsequently drowned.

Probably a mating dispute, Keyes concluded wryly as he got out his pen and began to do the crossword puzzle. As he brought to bear his concentration on the first clue, music suddenly surged out of the speaker directly over his head. So surprised was he by what he heard that he forgot to be grouchy about its volume, and also forgot to remain uninterested. Pounding unnaturally– in *this* place– was the opening movement from Carl Orff's *Carmina Burana*; true, a heavy electronic beat had been grafted to it, but even so, the wild pagan music and the Latin chants were not what you would call standard stripping fare. Keyes looked to the stage as the routine began.

The young woman– perhaps not even twenty– was very beautiful, and already stark naked, which in itself was as unusual as her selection of backing soundtrack. He could not get a good look at her face, as she had very long and very black, straight hair, which she was attempting to manipulate as if the thick strands were the fabled seven veils. She whirled her hair around her breasts, which seemed quite large because she herself was no more than five feet tall, and small-waisted; she did many other things with her hair and body, and Keyes found her attempt at something vaguely artistic endearing. The rest of the men in the bar, however, did not. As they began to boo and hiss at her efforts, she stopped suddenly and glared out, at first defiantly, but then Keyes saw her begin to play in an agitated fashion with the strands of hair drifting along her left thigh.

He had seen such a motion before, and recently... he leaned forward, and began to dress her with his eyes– it *was* her; the girl in the sequined outfit who had been kissing Alan Wales not long before Wales died.

(3:4) Along the Avon River

By the time Keyes left The Gilded Lily, the rain had diminished to a fine mist, the kind of gentle but persistent drizzle that he imagined thanes had to deal with on a regular basis. It bothered him that the suffering of thanes is what he imagined. He did not want to imagine or even think any more about Scottish Plays, their weather and their consequences. Unfortunately, Keyes was incapable of getting the bloody business out of his mind.

"The Balls?" he suggested to himself in half a voice, glancing in that direction. It was not yet three o'clock– too early for drinking, even though he had already had what he rounded off not very honestly as "a couple of beers." He knew what was likely to happen if he went into another pub now.

Instead he set off walking, aimlessly. Almost as soon as he began to move, he felt better, even if he didn't think much more clearly. As he trudged along, skirting puddles of water and patches of mud, Keyes took note of what he had noticed before about Stratford– how it resembled a theatre itself in a certain way: the storefronts in the core, in almost every case, were very beautiful and well designed; once in a while there were even small masterpieces of consumer-friendly aesthetics. However, once one stepped into an alley or onto a side-street, behind the scenes, so to speak, a more ordinary city appeared: clotheslines hung with laundry were strung between buildings badly in need of renovation, or coats of paint; green plastic garbage bags lay scattered about, some ripped apart by prowling wildlife. Rain-softened earth squished beneath Keyes' shoes, and his nostrils were full of an odour combining decayed refuse with frying onions and automobile exhaust.

Illusion and reality, Keyes thought, Mutt and Jeff, as he stepped around a broken beer bottle, brown shards of which were strewn across a torn copy of the program for *Medea*.

Lost in such thoughts, Keyes did not notice that his feet had made their way without his help back toward the Festival theatre. He realized what was happening to him only when the spiky mass of the building loomed at the end of a tree-lined street.

"Avaunt," he growled goofily, "and quit my sight!"

To be sure that it did, he made a sharp left turn and stalked down toward the river.

The Avon is not the stream it has been made to seem in promotional brochures about Stratford. A system of dams and weirs downstream from the main part of town, and most particularly, downstream from the theatre, have made it into a sizeable pond which patriotic townsfolk at one time or another dubbed Lake Victoria.

Her again, Keyes thought as he usually did when he encountered the Queen of Jubilees. Why must it always be her?

Still, the lake was pretty enough with its borders of softwood trees, most of them bending over the water and trailing parts of themselves in it, as Pre-Raphaelite girls might bend and trail their sleeves. By the time he reached Lake Victoria's phony but picturesque banks, Keyes was in an almost lyrical frame of mind.

Then he remembered the swan. The newspaper had blamed the death of the bird on a territorial squabble. Keyes knew swans to be thoroughly disagreeable creatures, at least on some occasions. He had seen a swan stop the charge of a large black dog, stop him dead in his tracks and so abruptly that the dog rolled over backwards. And this the swan had done merely by rising to its full height and displaying its wings, thereby transforming itself from something that must have reminded the marauding dog of a rather large duck into an exterminating angel seven feet high and just as wide.

"I suppose it wouldn't be pretty," Keyes told himself, "a fight between two bull swans..."

But was it a bull swan, he wondered, or a cock swan, or whatever it is that swan males are called? The paper hadn't sexed the bird, or gendered it. The report was too pristinely journalistic for such details.

Still thinking of swans and their dramas, Keyes sat down on a bench. It was wet, but he didn't really mind. The day was mild and the damp across his rump seemed somehow appropriate to it. Sitting there, he noticed that one of his shoe-laces was coming undone. He bent forward to tie it, and as he did so an airborne feather settled between his feet. It was white– a swan feather.

"I don't believe it," Keyes said, but believe it or not he reached out and collected the bit of fluff in his hand.

And now he saw something still more unbelievable. Just where the feather had lain, there was a tiny silver star.

"Last night," he murmured, "there were stars."

He had forgotten them, the little bright bits that he had found between the head of Alan Wales' and the head of the Bard of Avon.

Keyes relaxed his fingers, and the swan feather quickened on the light breeze and continued its journey. Then he picked up the silver sequin. He was sure it was the same.

What had he done with the others?

He rummaged in his jacket pocket among the house keys and theatre tickets. When he drew the hand out again he had lint between his fingers. He also had a sequin. It was the twin of the one he had just found on the banks of dear old Lake Victoria.

From the notebook of Jean-Claude Keyes:

Sometimes I believe that many of the seemingly intricate problems of being exist solely because God had too big a production budget and couldn't resist using it to load reality with an overabundance of brightly coloured bells and whistles whose only real effect is obfuscation. Viewed uncritically, our lives are a façade of multicoloured murk... but just because it's murky doesn't mean it's deep, as a lady once dear to me used to say. And death? Just God's way, like Shakespeare's, of clearing the stage when all else fails.

(3:5) The Jester's Bells

All streets in Stratford, in the end, led to The Jester's Bells, at least all streets roamed by actors, and so Keyes found himself there at the end of the day, having a light supper and feeling, if not better, at least more fit to socialize.

There were a great many customers over the dinner hour, most of them tourists as far as Keyes could tell, and these all disappeared as if by magic at around 7:30, half an hour before curtain time. The atmosphere went through a subtle change as the lights were dimmed, which enhanced the muted pastel colours of the walls and the varnished woods; decorative stained-glass panels above the bar brightened perceptibly, green, red and gold, and cigarette smoke whirled lazily in orbit around the ceiling fans. Soon, off-work Festival employees began to come in through both the front and back entrances, and within the hour, it seemed to Keyes that everyone who wasn't on or backstage was in the pub; and all were drinking heavily. The words "Wales" and "murder" buzzed about like undisciplined pixies, interrupting and underscoring every conversation.

Anyone who knew Keyes even slightly sought him out, bought him a drink, and asked him what had happened, what it had been like, what he thought about it. Some of the drinks he accepted, and some of the questions he tried to answer, or theorize about, but mostly his side of the dialogue consisted of shrugs and head-shaking.

"Do you think he'd been dead long?"

"Was it, like, you know... *really* messy?"

"Was Wales robbed?"

"Did the cops give you a rough time?"

"Who...?"

"What...?"

"Where...?"

"How...?"

"When...?"

"Why...?"

It was with a great deal of relief that Keyes finally saw Seamus O'Reilly elbowing his way through the smoke and chatter; he had Sandra on his arm. O'Reilly spotted Keyes and waved for him to join them in a vacant high-backed booth near an ancient Rockola jukebox which had been recently renovated and moved into the bar. (This jukebox was not so offensive as some, since it contained solely a wide selection of blues music, both country blues from the Mississippi Delta, and city blues of the Chicago hue.) Keyes excused himself from his current knot of inquisitors, picked up his beer mug, and a moment later seated himself beside Sandra.

The waitress, Julia, appeared in a puff of efficiency.

"Strong drink!" O'Reilly demanded, handing her some coins as he spoke. "And put some music on for us, my dear, to shield our discourse from prying ears!"

Julia complied, and soon after the air was filled with the voices of old blind black men with old guitars, gossiping about women and whiskey and the retribution of the Devil.

Seamus O'Reilly, for his part, wanted to gossip about the police, and Alan Wales.

"The *garda* were waiting for me at the stage door," he said. "I still had my make-up on when they invited me down to the station to assist them with their investigation; that's how the British Bobbies refer to it. They also suggested quite strongly that I improve my attitude."

"Why would they say that?" Keyes asked.

"Well, I suppose I must have laughed... I think I said 'about time,' or some such thing, as well." O'Reilly seemed to have overcome the horror he had experienced in the physical presence of the body.

"I see their point– the police are apt to be over-sensitive to someone who finds murder a source for amusement; they're funny that way. I wonder if they investigate swans?" Keyes said.

"What have swans got to do with anything? Anyway, I guess they brought me in first because somebody overheard me say something unkind about Mr. Wales at a party; something involving unpleasant and inventive forms of torture and termination; there's quite a long list of people they'll be interviewing for expressing precisely the same sentiments. Anyway, I told them I hated the bastard– I'm sorry, Sandra, that's the way it was– but I didn't kill him. You know, Claude, I'm thinking about setting up a lottery or something to pick whoever did it, maybe with some kind of reward..."

"*That'll* please the cops."

"Fuck them. In Ireland– "

"You haven't been within spitting distance of Ireland in thirty-five years!"

"Beside the point. Whose side are you on?"

"Yours, but that's beside the point, too." Keyes glanced sidelong at Sandra, to see how she was reacting to this disparagement of her late lover; sometimes O'Reilly rode roughshod over other people's emotions, even people he cared about, so carried away did he become with the strength of his own. Seamus had been an actor too long, Keyes thought, to have any real insight into character, or rather any insight into real character.

Sandra might as well have been onstage, deep into a role and unaffected by the small concerns of the mundane world around her. She stared at some point in the middle distance, a vague half-smile turning up the corners of her mouth. However, Keyes noticed something that perhaps only six other people in the world knew about Sandra Edel.

On her right hand she wore, as always, her most treasured possession, a large paste-and-pewter ring which had been part of her costume as Vittoria Corombona; the director of *The White Devil* had presented the ring to her as a gift on closing night, many years ago. When she was extremely upset or extremely happy, she had the habit of twisting the ring a quarter turn round her finger every few seconds; she was doing so now, and as she did, the lamplight over their booth caught it. The ring flashed briefly and brilliantly, and Keyes thought of stars, of sequins. Then he noticed that the ring had suffered some extensive damage to the stone; it was almost cracked in half.

"...and if Wales hadn't been such a– "

Sandra spoke then, cutting O'Reilly off in mid-sentence; she was one of the few people in the company brave or foolhardy enough to do such a thing.

"Please, Seamus," she said. "You know how I hate listening to notes at the end of the show. He's dead. There's nothing anyone can do. Let's talk about something else, something real..." She took a small sip of her wine. "I got my contract offer today, for next year. It's insulting, really. Perhaps it's time for me to move on. It's been far too long since I worked in Europe."

"Maybe you shouldn't be too hasty," O'Reilly began. "Our Byron project..."

Keyes excused himself to use the washroom. One of the aspects of theatre life, as least in Stratford, which he had particularly hated, was the fact that whenever two actors met, the conversation almost always turned to money, or how badly they were being treated, or both. It seemed that it held true even now, with Death prominent in the wings.

Raw-edged blues followed him through the pub:

Gotta keep movin', gotta keep movin'–
There's a hellhound on my trail...

Keyes saw George Brocken standing next to the bar, cradling a cup of steaming black coffee in both hands, his gaze shifting here and there around the room he had helped design as a favour to the owner; his expression indicated that he was perhaps criticizing his own taste, wondering where he had erred. Keyes nodded to him, although he really only knew him through his work. Grace Lockhardt stood beside him–Brocken was known to spend time with those who had most hands-on dealings with his creations: the cutters, the dyers, and the dressers. Grace was staring in the direction of the booth Keyes had just quitted.

Keyes passed by Betty, who was somewhat unsteadily putting on her raincoat.

"Claude!" she said, "I'm glad I ran into you– do you have your house keys with you? I locked mine in the basement this morning and haven't had time to deal with retrieving them."

Shaking his head, Keyes handed them over. In the process, one of Keyes' fingers picked up a minute silver highlight, which Betty commented upon:

"New fashion statement, Claude?"

"No," he replied. "Just new mysteries. See you later, Betty."

"Well, *you've* certainly gotten enigmatic since yesterday," she said to Keyes' back.

Keyes mumbled, "So I have," in agreement to this observation as he entered the men's room. Hobart Porliss was just leaving his post at a urinal.

"Keyes," he said, and nodded.

"Porliss," Keyes nodded in return, and that was the extent of their exchange. Though the two men had worked together as actors years before, they were not particularly well-acquainted, and their shared experience with Wales' corpse had not altered the relationship; if anything, it gave them more reason than ever to avoid one another's company. Porliss was not known for his love of writers. Too often he had been attacked by them; too often they had got in the way of his vision of how things ought to be done. Even Shakespeare got in his way sometimes, as Keyes had noticed during this current production of *Macbeth*. Keyes, for his part, had heard

Porliss gossiping about him at a party once. Porliss had called him a "turncoat" for leaving the stage to become a writer. It bothered Keyes that he too felt this about his defection, on certain days at least.

On the way back, he noticed a top hat sitting upside down on the bar.

"What's that for?" he asked Bruno.

"The hat?" Bruno said, putting aside the glass he was polishing. "We're having a pool."

"What sort of a pool?" Keyes asked obligingly.

"For Wales' murderer. The police don't have a clue– literally. Lots of motives, and lots of suspects. Practically everybody who knew the guy is a suspect. But there's no evidence against anybody."

"I still don't get it."

Bruno grinned. "We're going to let Lady Luck tell us who did it, or Dame Fortune as O'Reilly calls it– I got the idea from him."

He pushed a small pad of notepaper across the bar toward Keyes.

"Put your name down," he said, "and fold the paper twice. Then put it in the hat."

"I didn't kill Wales," Keyes said. He was feeling uneasy all of a sudden.

"I didn't say you did," Bruno continued. "But the idea is to see what Lady Luck says."

"That's crazy."

"So don't play. Everyone else who comes in here is playing, but if you don't want to, then don't. It'll look funny, though."

Keyes frowned and glanced into the hat. It was filled almost to the brim with little pieces of paper folded twice. Bruno held out a ballpoint pen to him.

"Oh, what the hell," Keyes said, as he took the pen.

"My sentiments exactly," Bruno said.

Keyes wrote his name on the paper, folded it as he had been instructed, and tossed it in the hat.

"Not a *nom de plume*, I hope," Bruno said.

"The real McCoy," Keyes assured him. "I'm happy to see you're not overcome with grief, anyway."

Bruno gave an expressive shrug of his thin shoulders. "The conceited little fucker ruined three dartboards with his Jim Bowie routine, and almost drilled a couple of customers... call me heartless, call me a cold fish– or just call me Bruno."

Keyes turned to leave.

"Wait a minute," Bruno called after him.

Keyes looked back. The bartender had another hat in his hand. This time it was a sombrero of the sort that tourists bring home from trips to Mexico or other places south of the border.

"What's that for?"

"It's for the money," Bruno said. "You owe me a dollar."

"A dollar! What for?"

"After Lady luck has fingered the murderer, we're going to present him with the money we collect."

"Or her," Keyes added.

"Right. Or her."

"But what for? As a prize for getting rid of Wales? That's not funny."

Bruno shook his head. "You said it, not me. The money is to help with the defence– legal fees are *really* murder!"

Keyes couldn't help laughing. He fished a loonie out of his pocket and laid it on the bar. He liked spending loonies. He even liked giving them away. The dollar coin with the Northern Loon on it seemed to him a genial invention, perhaps the most genial of all Canadian inventions, and was rumoured to be an endangered species, perhaps to be supplanted by etchings of the Parliament buildings.

"You hustled me, Bruno."

"Not me," Bruno said. "Lady Luck, maybe, or Dame Fortune, but never me."

Without seeming to look at it, Bruno scooped up the coin and dropped it into the sombrero. As it joined its fellows, Keyes' loonie made the merry clink that loonies are wont to make.

Upon returning to his companions, before they saw him, Keyes overheard O'Reilly finishing what sounded like a major pronouncement:

"– and you would have been far better off with Claude, or even with *me*, for that matter!"

Sandra made no reply, but Keyes saw that she was twisting the phony, broken ring a trifle more vigorously.

Suddenly, the limited floor space beside the table was filled, as if by magic, by a quartet of blue-haired ladies in identical tailored suits; each had a small name tag on her lapel, and each clutched a program in her tiny hand. They were staring at Seamus O'Reilly with something like lust in their eyes.

"Mr. O'Reilly," said one of them nervously, "we don't want to intrude, but we're from Illinois and we come here every year, and... well, we've been big fans of yours for just ages..."

O'Reilly flashed Keyes a "Succour me!" look, which Keyes ignored with a large grin.

"Let's go over to the bar," Keyes said. "Seamus will be busy for a while."

Sandra nodded. "And that waitress takes forever."

"Look at this crowd," Keyes said in Julia's defence. "She's doing her best."

It was not Sandra's way to be generous to waitresses, or younger women, for that matter, unless they could be counted among her admirers.

"Hello, Bruno, darling," Sandra said, taking the only free stool at the bar. Keyes hovered close behind her.

"Sandra!" Bruno exclaimed as enthusiastically as if she had just appeared on the set of *I Puritani* wearing a crimson dress. And then, in a flat voice: "Hello again, Claude."

"Oh, what shall I drink, Bruno?" Sandra wondered.

"Name it, Sandra, and I'll do whatever it takes to provide."

Sandra thought for a moment. "What are you having, Claude?"

"I'll stay with beer."

"Too dreary. Bruno, mix me a Stinger. I need something to clear my head."

"A Stinger ought to do the trick," Bruno said.

He turned away to his work, and as soon as he did, Sandra's mood changed. She became suddenly pensive and completely unaware of Keyes' continuing attention.

Bruno turned again, and caught Sandra brooding.

"Hey, where did *you* go?" he asked.

Sandra brightened immediately. "Me? Oh... well, if you must know, I was in Venice. Do you remember, Claude?"

"Of course," Keyes said shortly. Their trip to Venice had begun as the dream of love for which Venice is famous, and ended in a shouting match in which Sandra did the lioness' share of the shouting. For Keyes, Venice meant the beginning of the end of their affair. He always remembered it with discomfort bordering on pain.

"Have you been to Venice, Bruno?" Sandra continued.

"I've been everywhere one time or another."

"Claude's still cross because I had a little flirtation while we were there."

Bruno put Sandra's drink before her. She sipped it, then smiled at him as if the drink was the best she had ever tasted.

"I'm not cross," Keyes said, "and I still want a beer."

"Of course you are, love. It's not as if I did anything with Turiddu..."

"Turiddu!" Bruno said. "Sicilian?"

"Why, yes, now that you mention it. He *was* Sicilian. Dark, gloriously dark... all Angus bull and raven."

"Oh, lord," Keyes muttered.

Again Sandra sipped her drink.

"What was a Sicilian doing in Venice?" Bruno wanted to know.

"Don't act dumb, Bruno," Keyes growled. "He was doing Sandra, or trying to."

"It wasn't like that at all," Sandra said indignantly. "All we did was slip away one afternoon to Torcello..."

O'Reilly appeared and pressed in between Keyes and Sandra.

"There you are, traitors! What's going on here?" he demanded. "Another conspiracy?"

Bruno grinned. "In the theatre, there are always conspiracies."

"You're damned right there are," O'Reilly said. "At the moment the conspiracy seems to be to cause my expiration by thirst."

Already the bottle of Irish whiskey was in Bruno's hand.

A boom of distant thunder rattled the walls of The Balls.

"I think I'll be on my way," Keyes said, rather than re-seating himself, "before the rain starts again..."

"Are you talking to yourself again?" O'Reilly wished to know.

"To anyone who'll listen, I suppose," Keyes said, stepping back from the bar and leaning to kiss Sandra lightly on the cheek. "If you need me for anything, you know where I am."

Sandra smiled in the sad way she had on certain occasions, and Keyes missed her very much, suddenly, in spite of Venice and everything in between.

"Thank you, Claude," she said. "You're a nice man."

"For all the good it does me..." he whispered as he wended his way to the exit.

(3:6) Ontario Street

Keyes stepped out into an operatic rainfall; even the word "torrent" was more woefully inadequate than Curly Joe Howard would have been, cast as King Lear. A few over-dressed tourists huddled beneath awnings and in doorways, probably wondering why the hefty ticket prices didn't include some sort of all-purpose weather insurance. After all, it was just a bit too much to be expected to boldly support the Arts in Canada, *and* get soaked to the bone for your cultural pains. The only active vehicles seemed to be cabs– Stratford, Keyes had noticed, had more taxis than it had doughnut shops, which, if you are at all familiar with the town, is quite a significant statistic. While it is possible to be disappointed here by a particular Portia or Benedict, or by your hotel accommodations, you can always get a taxi, with a double-dip cruller to munch along the way.

Keyes turned his collar up and hunkered down to present as small a target as possible to the elements. An impressive thunder-lightning combination joined the kettledrum rain, turning the whole scene into something perfectly Wagnerian. But, in his path was not Jon Vickers singing Siegfried; instead, on a bench by the curb, sitting quietly drowning in the downpour, was what looked to him like the saddest girl in the world.

Ophelia in T-shirt and jeans, Keyes thought as he approached her, drawn by the despair that hung around her as heavily as the rain. Her eyes were closed, and it wasn't rain that leaked from beneath the lids, down to a pouty mouth trembling with repressed sobbing. Her straight, black hair was plastered smooth against her face, neck and shoulders, and she hugged herself as she rocked from side to side. Something about her...

"Are you all right, Miss?" he asked, keeping well outside of the "personal space" he'd heard so much about. She responded with a silent and vigorous nod which meant, "Go away and leave me alone, you old fool."

Keyes did not go away. Ungenerous souls watching from windows might have suspected his creaking libido of unsavoury opportunism, but this was not so. His attitude was archaic, certainly, perhaps atavistic and a valuable lesson for all childless men of a certain age, but reprehensible it was not. Had he a daughter of his own, he would certainly want someone– even an old fool– to help her get in out of the rain, if only because even in this inventively damaged age, commonplace pneumonia could still be every bit as deadly as radioactive fallout or ultraviolet rays or overexposure to CBC situation comedies. And so he persevered with his ragged knight errant routine.

"You really should get inside," he said in a not terribly suave or authoritative voice. "The rain doesn't look like it's going to let up for a while..."

"Who cares?" she snapped back, with a mature viciousness he would have expected from someone who had experienced the full five Shakespearean acts of human suffering rather than the mere prologue her apparent age suggested.

"Well, I suppose *I* care, or I wouldn't have stopped to share this dry-land drowning experience, would I?"

She looked at Keyes straight on. It was the first time he'd seen her face clearly, but now that he thought about it, her shape was unmistakeable– she was the dancer from The Gilded Lily, Alan Wales'... friend? No wonder she wasn't worried about catching cold, he reflected– it was already an occupational hazard with her. He liked the face, more than the shape, which was a bit excessive for his tastes. She had thick black eyebrows, and near-black eyes as well; her cheekbones were high and pronounced; her lips were the same red as the dress she had worn the night before. A small scar ran down her left cheek– another occupational hazard?

"Look," he persisted, "come inside and I'll buy you a cup of coffee..."

"I can afford my own coffee... and I wouldn't go in *there* if the offer was for steak and champagne!" Her emphasis on "there" was the same "den-of-iniquity" pronunciation more often applied to *her* place of employment. Having made the attempt at altruism, Keyes was about to move on before anybody caught him at it, but the girl continued to speak, as if she couldn't help herself, as if it had all been pent-up and simply waiting for someone to ask.

"I know what they're up to in there, crying in their beer about how he'll be missed, about how much they respected him... but they all hated him!"

She wasn't talking to Keyes any more; she was addressing the rain, the cold wind, and the "they" inside the bar. And it was obvious to Keyes that the subject of her tears was Alan Wales. He could have corrected her impression of the attitudes inside the pub concerning Wales: the phrase "he'll be missed" was not among those he'd heard.

"Are you talking about Alan Wales?" he asked, if only to confirm his own deductive omniscience.

"You knew him?"

Keyes was becoming distinctly more uncomfortable by the second.

"I... it was me who found him... the body. I'm Claude Keyes."

She was on her feet before he'd finished the introduction. Her eyes widened slightly in recognition, with a slight flicker of unjustified fear.

"I've seen you before, in the bar– I thought you were just another horny old fart, but you're one of *them*, aren't you?" she said.

Before Keyes could disavow any membership in whatever club she was referring to with so much venom, the girl was gone, half-running off into the storm. Thunder applauded her exit, then a showy bolt of lightning struck a street light on the corner; there was an intense flickering, more thunder, and the entire block went dark.

(3:7) Betty's Bed & Breakfast

Keyes couldn't get the girl out of his mind– who was she to Hecuba, or Hecuba to her? Any liaison she might have had with Wales was unusual, to say the least. For all of their modern ways and open-minded acceptance of everything from actors to mutant turtles to Madonna, theatre people still maintained a kind of gypsy-clique style of living, not necessarily from snobbery (although this happens), but mostly for simplicity's sake: those who understand who you are and what you do are easiest to get along with on a day-to-day basis, intimately or otherwise.

But he could speculate fruitlessly all night on Wales' relationship with the rain-ridden stripper-girl... and the sequins she seemed to shed like a second skin; there was a much simpler way to find out what had gone on, since there was a horse's mouth close to hand.

Betty was sitting at the kitchen table sipping a cup of restorative tea when Keyes got back. She had obviously been hard at work– her bare arms and face were splotched with Titanium White and Hooker's Green. As usual however, there was not a spot of paint on her working clothes: pressed white jeans and an unwrinkled white T-shirt. Keyes believed it was a point of honour with her to paint her canvas and not her clothing.

After he had described his encounter to Betty, she sniffed as if someone in a plaid suit had been allowed through the front door.

"That one!" she said, reaching for the Scotch bottle beside the teapot, and splashing two fingers– thumbs, more like it– into her cup, while lighting a cigarette with the other hand; sometimes Keyes envied Betty her ambidextrous decadence.

"Are you going to tell me who she is," Keyes asked, "and what her sins are, or do I have to resort to blackmail by threatening to reveal a few things I haven't told anyone about you yet?"

"How much could *that* be? Leave me something for my memoirs, Claude. Her name is Janie– Janie Ellison, but she *dances* under the name of Kiri," Betty said. "She's an area girl– from St. Marys, I believe– and has quite a reputation around here. Shame, really. Somebody told me she has a beautiful mother whose heart she's breaking, a hard-working father... how dope and sleeping around and booze evolve out of such a solid heritage is beyond me. Makes me thankful *I'll* never have to deal with something like that! I have enough trouble with tourists, let alone children."

"Betty, can you be a little more specific? For example, what did this Janie Ellison have to do with Alan Wales, if anything?"

"Oh, she was one of his girls..."

"'One of his girls'? How un-'90s of you."

"I'm old-fashioned. It's part of my charm. No, really, Wales always kept a kind of groupie-harem around him, three or four on the string, sometimes. It's a character flaw in certain young actors– and some of the old ones, too."

Betty was also well-acquainted with Seamus O'Reilly. She continued.

"But as a rule, most of them keep their romances, if you can call them that, within the company, which, while incestuous, is quite wise and much less complicated in the long run. The 'lock-up-your-daughters' attitude is still very much alive in some places; Stratford, for example."

"Keep going."

"That's really about all I know, except that the girl was so obsessed by Wales that she dropped out of school, and ended up with this... *dancing* job. Wales was fond of making jokes about it at the bar, comments about how all her skills were oral ones, and he didn't mean declaiming Shakespeare. No one else thought his jokes were particularly funny. I thought about smacking him one night after one of his cracks that disgusted even me, but I was too drunk."

"But she still seems to care about him. How is it possible, after treatment like that?"

Betty shrugged.

"You're asking me? I barely understand how my microwave works, let alone other people's love lives."

"And that we have in common, my friend," Keyes said, hoisting his mug in her direction. "But I am beginning to understand the lack of deep and abiding sorrow over Wales' untimely departure, in every case but Ms. Kiri Ellison's."

"You're not going to get involved in all of this, are you?" Betty asked.

"I already *am* involved."

"Just because you found the body? It could have been anybody!"

"But it wasn't anybody– it was me."

"Claude, don't start that 'for whom the bell tolls' nonsense. Hasn't anyone pointed out to you lately what an unpleasant world this is? The bells stopped tolling a long time ago."

"No, they've just gotten so loud and constant that people have forgotten they exist. Like traffic noise and the moaning of starving millions." Keyes stood up. "Thanks for the information. Well, I should spend the evening working on my manuscript, maybe make it an early night."

"While you're at it you should work on curing this rampant sentimentalism you seem to be suffering from— it can't be good for your liver." Her voice was gentler than her words.

"It probably isn't," Keyes agreed, and left Betty Beardsley to her quiet battle with her own liver's nemesis.

Keyes awoke in the middle of the night, troubled. He tried his usual remedy for insomnia, work, but was unable to concentrate on his current chapter, which dealt with one of Seamus' four ex-wives. He went to the kitchen and sat there by candlelight smoking a cigarette over a glass of warm milk. After fifteen minutes of this therapy, Keyes yawned, extinguished his cigarette and candle, rinsed his milk glass, and returned to his own room.

This time he fell into sleep quickly... and equally quickly, plunged into the depths of a dream which he would remember until the end of his days. The dream went on and on, and was one of those in which he was aware that he was dreaming, but was unable to escape from it.

First, he saw the well on the Marquee deck, but the hole was three times as wide as in reality, and virtually bottomless.

The entire scene itself floated in some kind of star-speckled void. Loud thunder boomed and rolled like a great cosmic ocean. Out of the well floated Alan Wales, handsome and vital and laughing in echoing guffaws at three figures who stood around him.

The Keyes-who-dreamed knew somehow that he was looking at Three Murderers, and these were stock players from one of his earlier dreams– each one had the face of Claude Keyes. Wales' laughter was now almost as deafening as the thunder, and the first Keyes, as if unable to stand the laughing any longer, struck at Wales with a set of iron manacles which had appeared in Keyes' hands. Wales, still laughing, began to rotate in the air from the force of the blow, pinwheels of blood radiating from his spinning form.

The second Keyes seized the whirling body, and pinned it down, forcing the limbs into unnatural positions.

The third and final Keyes was suddenly in possession of the manacles, and began to run in leaping slow-motion strides to the river. It was a much cleaner and clearer river than the Avon had been for years– the stars were reflected in it.

Keyes flung the chains away from himself, and a fine spatter of blood rained from them as they whirled through the air toward the deepest part of the Avon River. But the heavy metal links landed upon a swan instead, wrapping themselves around its neck, and dragging the huge pale bird beneath the surface...

At last, the river disappeared. The stars went out, and Keyes saw his three selves fly through the air toward each other, to become one again. The spirit of Wales was gone.

Keyes was alone in the void.

(3:8) The Jester's Bells

Very late that night, slightly into morning of the next day, Grace Lockhardt sat on a stool in The Jester's Bells, quietly telling a mostly sympathetic George Brocken a great many of her hopes, her fears, her aspirations. Her make-up, not terribly subtle or effective at the best of times, was streaked with tear tracks, so that parts of her face resembled a dog-eared street map. The names "Sandra" and "Wales" came up frequently. When the well of her miseries became too deep for Brocken, he privately occupied his mind with one of his favourite mental exercises, that of redesigning the people around him, of clothing Grace more suitably (to his mind), re-styling her hair, and visualizing her in some far place, where she might be happier. Occasionally, Brocken's nose would wrinkle as Grace's perfume wafted across his face; it was an inexpensive scent which was supposed to suggest "the magic of a midsummer night," but made Brocken wonder only if Grace had recently fallen into a vat of fermented apricots.

From the jukebox behind them, a husky-voiced woman questioned, in less high-flown terms, the validity of continuing to exist without love in this troubled world.

(3:9) The Gilded Lily

Around the corner and down the street in The Gilded Lily, Kiri Ellison's thoughts were her own, as hidden and protected as her body was exposed. It was a rough crowd tonight, of truckers and factory labourers and drug dealers, and she was dancing to Guns 'N' Roses rather than Carl Orff, concentrating on giving the men what they wanted, as opposed to any experimentation with the limited form of her art.

What one of them wanted, just before last call, resulted in her being forced to explain her lack of interest to him with an open-handed punch. She left her surprised admirer on his leathered ass, blood spewing from a nose permanently altered.

(3:10) The apartment of Alessandra Edel

Sandra Edel was in her tower room across the river, walking back and forth through the apartment, wearing her favourite nightdress, a translucent blue affair of silk and lace. She was talking to herself, soliloquizing in the best tradition of her profession. There was no one there to applaud or criticize or hear at all, unless perhaps there was an audience of shades from the past lurking quietly in the stairwell.

From time to time, she would pick up the framed photograph of Alan Wales, and hold it at arm's length, frowning as if she was not quite sure who it was. Finally, she turned it face down on the table, and stood staring out the window, her lips still moving silently.

(3:11) The Necropolis

Alan Wales was laid to rest, as the saying goes, on Saturday morning. The weather was splendid, as the days of late autumn often are in southern Ontario. The sun shone gloriously; the crisp air had about it the zest of champagne. Stratford's Avondale Cemetery looked even more charming than it ordinarily did, and it was one of Canada's more charming graveyards. Only the solemn old evergreen trees and some tombstones, so mournful in both colour and attitude, kept the place from asking to be pressed into service as a set for *A Midsummer Night's Dream* or even *The Magic Flute*.

The grave was near the river, which was allowed to be itself this far downstream. The water in it moved slowly, meandering through a swamp of dead and dying trees—gnarled, twisted, blasted. Beavers might have made something useful and pleasant of it, had there been any beavers about. Rats liked it well enough, and birds. The dark copses were filled with birds, and on such a morning as this, they were singing their gaudy heads off.

Wales was fortunate in the neighbourhood that had been chosen for his eternity. The headstone closest to him was engraved with the name Death. Just beyond Death lay some-one called Peace.

I don't believe it, Keyes said to himself, when he read these grandiose stone labels. He went closer and discovered more information about the man named Death:

Arthur J. Death
1893 – 1969
R.I.P.

"Okay," Keyes mumbled. "Okay."

"What's that, Claude?" Betty said.

"Nothing. Talking to myself..."

Betty and Keyes had come together, and everyone else seemed to be there as well, or almost everyone, whether they wanted to be or not. Hobart Porliss had made a speech after the performance the night before, in which he urged the company to be at the funeral.

"Theatre tradition," Porliss had proclaimed, "demands our presence, regardless of what we personally thought of the deceased man."

O'Reilly stood a bit back and up the slope. It was the kind of position that he often found onstage– not in the centre or even in the front, but in a place where he could not be overlooked. Sandra stood close beside him, as she often had in recent days. She seemed almost to be sheltering in the lee of his bulk. Grace, for once, was conspicuously absent from Sandra's orbit. Porliss and Ziemski-Trapp, the Festival's Artistic Director, were at graveside with the rest of the company gathered about them.

The day was chosen so that members of the dead man's family, most of whom worked in factories or on the land, could attend. A few did. The Wales family stood on one side of the open grave; the company of *Macbeth* on the other. The two factions did not mix.

It had been something of a surprise to Keyes, and to almost everyone else who knew Wales, that his roots were just twelve miles or so from Stratford, in the small town of St. Marys, a fact which had come out in the course of arranging for the interment.

"He told *me* he was from Montreal," Betty had said.

"I thought he was born in England and emigrated here as a child," was O'Reilly's comment.

"Well, who would admit to being from St. Marys?" Porliss was heard to mutter.

None of the theatre people had turned up at the church service which had been held at an "evangelical" meeting house on the edge of town. A Reverend Wales was minister there, a cousin of Alan Wales. As a member of the family Reverend Wales had naturally been selected to preside at the graveside, even though his theatrical cousin had never thought of entering his church. The Reverend was a brittle individual in his forties who did his preaching, even at funerals, in a business suit of a painfully intense blue colour.

"Dearly Beloved..." he intoned, glowering across the coffin at the actors assembled beyond it, as if they were a coterie of demons rather than human beings.

Damnably Despised, Keyes thought, is what he means. It struck him as very strange that even here in the presence of death the truth could not be spoken. He wondered if the man in the blue suit trafficked much in truth. Somehow he did not think so.

Others were not so wary of plain speaking, of saying what they thought to be the truth at any rate.

"I knew something like this would happen," a woman shrilled, "if he took up with *them*!" Keyes noted how much her "them" resembled Kiri Ellison's.

The woman raised her hand Cassandra-like and pointed an accusing forefinger at the players. She was short and bulky and her blondined hair had been permed so violently that it resembled a scouring pad. She wore a great deal of make-up, very badly applied, and an aubergine trouser suit that can never have been in fashion, even in St. Marys, Ontario. Keyes took her to be the dead actor's mother, the Mater Dolorosa of this weird Passion Play.

She's not very old, Keyes thought sadly, surely not as old as Sandra, or even me. She must have had her son when she was hardly more than a child herself. The grief that she displayed was undoubtedly genuine.

"His mother?" Keyes whispered in Betty's ear.

Betty shrugged. "Certainly not *mine*."

The minister droned on for some time after the mother's outburst, skirting glibly around the circumstances of Wales' death, since the police had yet to release that information, assuming they even knew. Eventually, the Reverend invited Hermes Ziemski-Trapp, "Alan's employer," to say a few words.

"A few words!" Betty groaned. "I heard him give 'a few words' at the art gallery once– we were there for hours and missed last call!"

Ziemski-Trapp did blather on, but not so long as Betty had feared.

"We shall not know his like again," Ziemski-Trapp said finally, as Keyes, and no doubt everyone else in the actors' group, had known he would. Ziemski-Trapp was nothing if not predictable.

The minister called upon members of the funeral party to pray. Heads were bent and an archaic prayer of great form and little content was said, words that flew up, perhaps, although most of the mourners' thoughts remained below.

"Could that really have been his mother?" Betty asked Keyes as the two were walking back toward the centre of town. "She wasn't very old. She looked old because of all that paint and those clothes, but she wasn't."

"No, she wasn't."

"And it seems she loved him."

"Betty, we have just established that she was his mother. Mothers are supposed to love their sons."

"You sound suspiciously like that quaint preacher."

Keyes wondered if he did. The grand banality of death was difficult to avoid.

"Are you coming back to the house?" Betty said. "I'll give you tea."

Keyes thought it a bit early in the day for her tea.

"No, thanks," he said. "I've some shopping to do."

"All those women," Betty said as she wandered off. "What did they see in him? Even his mother..."

There was one more mourner at Alan Wales' funeral, but Keyes did not see her until he passed through the exit gate, because she had hung far back from both groups, had been almost hidden behind a marble monument, a grim, blindfolded angel of some kind. It was Kiri Ellison. She was dressed appropriately for the occasion, insofar as colour was concerned, at least: her spike-heeled shoes were black, her net stockings and tiny skirt were black, and her leather jacket the same, except for the glinting of metal studs and links of chain; even her lipstick seemed to be black, as far as Keyes could tell from this distance.

"The Dark Lady of the Sonnets?" Keyes said to a passing squirrel. Then he remembered something Betty had told him: this girl, too was from the same mythical place called St. Marys.

From the notebook of Jean-Claude Keyes:

Well, that's the end of it, for most of us at least, certainly for me. I didn't even know Wales, except in his final role as corpse. And now that corpse is buried, last rites administered.

But I have to admit the whole thing still fascinates me. I can't stop thinking about Kiri Ellison, and her dead paramour, and about Sandra. I should be over her.

These things keep going round in my head, round and round in a dozen different dialects and metres and forms. Kiri and Wales especially... how did they fit together– the girl naked before strangers and the boy hidden from them under pounds of make-up and fabric. The strangers who had watched Wales were of a different order, of course... or were they? A different slice of society, maybe, but voyeurs are voyeurs, whether they're in strip joints or the grandest of theatres. And we're all voyeurs...

Sandra, mature and glamorous, with such a capacity for love– how did she get mixed up, and mixed up so seriously, with a brute like Wales?

What am I to think? Where's the dramatic shape, the artistic symmetry of such relationships? If it's there, *I* can't see it. And why do I feel that there should be anything as comforting as symmetry, anyway?

In the end, Betty is right– it's none of my business and there's no reason I should lose any sleep over it. Wales' death will be dealt with by the police, and will probably have a very simple explanation, as ninety-nine percent of murders do. The killer will be caught, tried, and fade away in prison...

Most of us will get over it quickly enough. It's just a matter of repairing the damage done to our cages by the brief rattling, using whatever tools we have...

But Sandra? Dramatic scenes can't solve all of our problems. And Kiri Ellison? What's going to happen to a kid like that? What's she got to look forward to but disease or dope or alcoholism, or all of them...? to dying alone and unloved...

Jesus, Claude, get a grip.

ACT FOUR

As Cast

They say this town is full of cozenage;
As, nimble jugglers that deceive the eye,
Dark-working sorcerers that change the mind,
Soul-killing witches that deform the body,
Disguised cheaters, prating mountebanks,
And many such-like liberties of sin...
– *The Comedy of Errors,* Act I, Scene 2

(4:1) Along the river-bank, and York Lane

Keyes had no shopping to do, in fact, but he was too restless to sit still in one place, especially if Betty stayed in whatever mood this was that made her want to speculate on the nature of motherly love.

Besides, the day continued to be fine. It was a day for strolling esplanades and boardwalks beside the sea. The closest approximation in Stratford was the lakeside, and that is where Keyes strolled. After a little of this he decided to stroll around the whole of it.

"How long will it take, I wonder, to circumnavigate Lake Victoria?" he asked himself in a voice he had borrowed from Seamus O'Reilly, a voice O'Reilly used only when the old actor was cast as a lord, a gentleman, or an attendant. Keyes realized of course that he wasn't really circumnavigating, but the word was too attractive not to use.

His energy was high, which rather puzzled him, as he had not slept well the night before; it also did not seem proper that funeral-going should give him such a lift. Wherever the vigour came from, it put a spring in his step. Probably it was just the weather.

He passed the island where the dead swan had been found, then the bench where he had come across the star sequins. They continued to trouble him, those sequins did. They made him suspect possibilities that he wished he could believe were impossible.

Then he passed the theatre. One of its flags was flying at half-mast. Based on what Keyes had learned so far, it was more than Alan Wales deserved.

He continued on to the Gallery Stratford, and to the golf course, although by then he had left Lake Victoria behind. Some jovial golfers were on their way from the clubhouse to the links.

"Links," he murmured aloud. "There must be links somewhere."

If there were, he didn't have them. He watched the golfers almost enviously, something he had never done before, then turned back toward the lake, the theatre, and Dead Swan Isle, as he had come to think of Tom Patterson Island.

"You're losing it, Keyes," he said. "I should have had a cup of Betty's high-test tea after all."

Now he quickened his pace slightly, realizing that his route along the banks of the Avon had taken him onto what was, for the most part, private property; he was crossing the back yards of expensive riverfront real estate, but, perhaps because of the ever-present roving bands of tourists, security was not so tight in Statford as it might be in other communities.

He arrived at the dam below the lake. It was one of his favourite places in town; he wasn't sure why. Perhaps it was the sound of water rushing through the floodgates, or perhaps the sense he had of the power of water pent up.

The funeral came into his mind again, and then the succession of sinister events that led up to it. All this was pent up in his mind, this lakeful of detail, waiting for some internal floodgate to be opened.

For a while Keyes studied the rushing water, then he sighed and turned away. Facing him was York Lane, a short gauntlet of small but up-scale shops. It occurred to him that he might do some shopping after all, or some browsing, if only to save himself from having lied to Betty.

In First Folio Books, it amused him to see a clerk packing away a dozen of the iron Shakespeare busts such as the one which seemed to have been guiding Alan Wales on his journey to Hades. Noticing his interest, the exuberant young man grinned widely and raised one of them, as if he were Hamlet with Yorick's skull.

"Gruesome, isn't it? Bad buy— we're returning them all!" His tone of voice indicated to Keyes that banishing the small monstrosities was the high point of the clerk's summer.

Keyes came away from the Señor Coffee store next door with the gratification that a cup of good espresso can provide. He glanced over baby clothes, the dresses in the fashion boutique, the yarn in the knit shop, and the chocolate truffles in a mysterious little place called Tid-Bits, and managed to resist the wares offered by all of them.

He was not so fortunate when he came to a shop called Smoke and Mirrors. This emporium seemed to deal in old stage properties. It was hung with *papier mâché* masks, posters, random bits of drapery. All its furnishings were painted, often in *faux-marbre*. There were boxes and bins of portfolios. Not since his visit to Sandra's apartment had he seen so much stagy stuff. Despite the glory of the sunshine, Keyes opened the door and went in.

It took his eyes a moment to adjust to the gloom of the shop's interior, and still another moment for them to tell him that he was the only customer there. He could see nothing as ordinary as a counter, but two women turned their heads in his direction as he approached. They were seated in armchairs, chatting quietly, and in a fashion that seemed to him entirely unbusinesslike, which warmed him to them immediately, taking them to be the staff of Smoke and Mirrors. Both women were tall and dark and beautiful. They were also graceful when they stood up and gracious when they spoke, which they did in a curious kind of alternation.

Like Tweedledee and Tweedledum, Keyes thought, no matter how little the women of Smoke and Mirrors resembled Carroll's twins.

"Can we help you?" said Smoke– as he now came to think of her– with brisk and efficient courtesy.

"Just browsing," Keyes replied, thinking as he said it that it might be very pleasant to be helped one way or another by just such a lady.

"Let us know if there's something we can show you," said Mirrors, more vaguely than her partner, but in a manner that was equally as friendly.

"Thank you," Keyes said. Perhaps I might see just one more centimetre of exquisitely tanned flesh?

Immediately after this he thought, I really am losing it. I'm getting to be as crazy as everybody else in this outrageous town.

He poked about in a corner where some stage weapons had been stacked, long-handled polearms such as halberds and partisans. The women settled in their chairs and resumed their quiet conversation, which was about Alan Wales.

"He was in here only the day before," Smoke said. "Didn't buy anything of course."

"He never did... buy anything, I mean," Mirrors said.

"He asked me what time I finished work."

"You, too?"

"Oh, yes. The old 'what's-a-goodlooking-girl-like-you-doing-in-a-joint-like-this' routine. Very tacky."

"Rather beautiful though," Mirrors murmured dreamily.

"More than that... excessively beautiful. But tacky. Very, very tacky."

Keyes moved further away, far enough to be kept from hearing the substance of what the two women were saying. He found some portfolios filled with drawings made by costume designers and began to rummage through them. A fine Desmond Heeley caught and held his attention, then an exquisite Sam Kirkpatrick. With great pleasure he went through one portfolio and opened another. The first drawing in it was by George Brocken.

Had Brocken been at the funeral? Keyes asked himself. He couldn't be sure, but he didn't remember seeing him. The more he thought about it, the more certain he became. Almost everyone had been there... but not Brocken.

He looked again at the drawing. It was one of the designs for *Macbeth*, a reject certainly, one of the many the designer might have prepared before finding just the right combination of colours and textures. It was labelled: Jerzy Cole as Fleance.

The next drawing was of Alan Wales in his Act I, Scene 2 appearance– Wales as the bleeding sergeant.

A small, many-footed shudder crept up Keyes' spine. It was very unsettling to be holding in his hands a drawing of the corpse he had found only a few days before. Except for the lighting, Brocken's design captured the scene exactly. The legs were spread in the same way; the hands and arms gestured with the same dramatic emphasis. It might have been an artist's sketch of "the scene of the crime" from the pre-photography era, or a heightened version of the police chalk outlines which mark where a corpse has lain. All the sketch lacked was the bust of Shakespeare and the blood.

Keyes put the drawing back and closed the portfolio. Slowly the eeriness of his discovery passed away. He had had enough of Smoke and Mirrors, however. He wanted to be back outside again, out in the bright autumn sunshine.

The two dark women watched him as he made his exit, which was precipitous, almost as if he were bolting, as a horse bolts when it is suddenly frightened.

"He was a weird one," Smoke said to Mirrors.

"Aye," Mirrors said to Smoke. "That he were."

(4:2) The Festival Theatre, a rehearsal hall

The date of the funeral fell on the same day as the Ricardo Benefit Cabaret, an annual event now in its third year. Ticket and liquor sale proceeds went to the Guthrie Award fund, in memory of a young actor who had died of AIDS four years earlier, after a long and brave struggle. Ricardo had been well-liked and respected by all who knew him, both as artist and human being. Entertainment, music, and dancing were scheduled, as Ricardo himself had loved these things; and he had requested, a few days before his death, that if he were to be remembered it should be in such a fashion.

It was decided to go ahead with the cabaret as planned, and word had come from Ziemski-Trapp that Wales was to be mentioned and made part of the event, for this year at least, and that a suitable gravity was to be adopted. O'Reilly saw the cabaret in the great Irish tradition of the wake, and scoffed at the concept of "suitable gravity" on the grounds that some of the best times, biggest hangovers, and most memorable romantic dalliances of his life had been the direct result of wakes. O'Reilly even volunteered to act as bartender for the night (performers and staff donated their time and talents), but no one trusted him in charge of the booze, although he was not told this directly. The organization committee– which consisted mainly of Grace Lockhardt– politely declined the offer of his services on the grounds that only union bartenders from the Festival staff were allowed to serve at such functions. It did not escape O'Reilly's notice that Bruno from The Bells popped up behind the bar from time to time, helping out when things got hectic.

A rehearsal hall on the top level of the Festival theatre had been taken over for the Ricardo Cabaret. The cavernous room was dominated by a replica of the main thrust-stage, on which the actors could practice their paces. Tonight, however, the mock stage was to host a variety of musical groups, skits, and speeches; part of the area in front of the stage was bare, to serve as a dance floor, and small tables were dotted elsewhere, complete with checkered table-cloths and candles stuck in wine bottles. A bar and hors d'oeuvres table guarded the entrance doors.

The function did not begin until 10:30 p.m., since most of the company and crew could not attend until the evening performances were over, but special permits and dispensations had been sought out in order that it could continue until the early hours of the morning. Keyes arrived at about midnight, and the room was nearly full to capacity. Many in the crowd had not even bothered to remove their stage make-up. One of the bands was in full swing, playing aggressive and loud rock and roll. Keyes grinned to himself, thinking of Betty– this music would drive her crazy, and she would probably spend half the night trying to get somebody to turn down the volume.

Keyes wanted to talk to George Brocken. In fact he felt he had to talk to him. The costume drawing he had seen at Smoke and Mirrors had worked strangely on his imagination since he saw it. The drawing suggested... he didn't quite know what. He had to talk to Brocken.

At first he had trouble finding the designer.

"Have you seen George Brocken?" he asked Hobart Porliss as the plump director waddled past.

"George? Oh yes, frequently." And then he was gone, lost from view in the midst of a crowd of boozy Thespians.

Keyes tried O'Reilly, too.

"Brocken? Over by the bar. I'm headed that way myself."

Together Keyes and O'Reilly went to the bar. Together they had a drink. Brocken was not there.

Sandra and Grace appeared, arm in arm, and dressed almost identically, which made a very strange effect. The short jacket, long skirt, and black boots, Keyes noticed, made Sandra look like a White Russian countess. The same outfit made Grace look uncomfortable.

"I saw him earlier," Sandra said. "Maybe he's gone home? What do you want him for?"

"I saw a drawing of his that interested me," Keyes explained not very candidly.

"Well, if you want to buy it, don't bother. He hates doing business, especially after hours."

"No, it's not that," Keyes said. "I'm not a collector. I just wanted to ask him some questions."

"George doesn't really care much for answering questions, either," Sandra observed.

Keyes spotted Betty, who was standing at the edge of the dance floor glaring at the musicians. It seemed a good idea to avoid her for the moment, as she would be in a foul mood until she had forced a change in music. There was a coffee urn near the bar, and Keyes poured himself a cup, then found an empty table in a dim corner, from where he could comfortably observe the proceedings. He watched Sandra whenever he could find her among the dancers and drinkers.

After a while, his stomach announced to him with a loud rumble that it was interested in whatever was going on over at the snack table. He found himself in a disorganized line-up, containing acquaintances and strangers (including Betty, who had abandoned her musical crusade) temporarily bound by the primal urge of hunger. George Brocken was not among these.

"I can eat it," said someone at Keyes' shoulder, someone speaking with a soprano voice, or in falsetto, "but I don't hanker after it."

"The pickled squid?" A tenor– a lighting designer named De Soto– said, not without a hint of superiority. "Step aside then and make way for those who do."

"Try the eggplant, love," a contralto voice suggested from somewhere not too far away. Keyes recognized Sandra in it, but when he turned to see her, she was gone.

"And the *heli skaras*," rumbled O'Reilly's baritone.

"*Lei, non troppo malo lei stesso*," an actress wearing fringe and little else playfully replied in pidgin Italian to something whispered into her ear by song-and-dance man Caspar Sax.

"What's that you're saying?" O'Reilly demanded.

"Italian, apparently, isn't your *forte*."

O'Reilly growled something incomprehensible and veered off toward the bar.

Irish, Keyes supposed, although he knew none of that curious tongue himself.

"Italian isn't my *forte* either," the fringed actress confided to Sax, "but I've managed nicely with my smattering of it on more than one *corso.*"

"I saw Billy while I was in Lausanne," the soprano said.

"What on earth is he doing in Lausanne?" asked De Soto, astonished.

"She."

"Oh, *that* Billy."

"Did you say 'Billy'?" Sax wondered.

"Surely *you* remember Billy."

"Oh yes. Bits of her, anyway..."

"Billy is the most extraordinary fund..." began Betty.

Ms. Fringe objected: "She's large, I know, but is 'fund' quite fair?"

"I was going to say, fund of curious information."

"That still sounds..."

"It was she," Betty persisted, "who told me about Blue Whales."

"Was that one of Alan's nicknames?" asked De Soto.

"Whales with an 'H,'" Betty explained impatiently. "The male of the species, Billy claims, has a penis three metres long."

"Three metres!" exclaimed in unison De Soto and Sax.

"Of course he keeps it hidden most of the time."

"Sly puss!" said a person from props with what seemed to be real appreciation.

"Has anyone seen George Brocken?" Keyes managed to say before these speculations on natural history continued.

Everyone spoke at once:

"Over by the bar..."

"Talking to Hobie..."

"Is he here tonight?"

Keyes thanked them and moved on. Hobart Porliss loomed before him.

"I agree with Robin," he was saying to Damian Pace. "Hangovers are often more interesting than the parties that bring them on."

"Robin makes me tired," the company's Macbeth grumbled. "He's perverse. He thinks too much."

"Some of us are less exacting, dear boy, than you."

Keyes asked his question again with results as confusing and useless as before. Then he saw O'Reilly again, talking to the Smoke and Mirrors women, whose names were actually Josephine and Francesca, and Julia, who was happily sipping drinks rather than serving them.

"I aspire..." Julia said almost soulfully.

"I know, I know!" Frankie, as she was called, sympathized.

"If only life were more like art," Jo put in. "The great geishas..."

"Oh lord!" said O'Reilly. "For God's sake let's have some *heli skaras*, if only to stop that gob."

He went off, ostensibly in search of the delicacy, but more likely seeking fresh Bushmill's.

"Barbarian!" Julia good-naturedly hissed after him.

"Speaking of the East," Jo said, perhaps to change the subject, "I had a letter from Io. Apparently she's leaving Pavel after all."

"At last!" Julia said. "She's finally tired of his affairs."

"Just tired of him, I think, or of herself with him, which is worse."

"Io and I crossed paths," Frankie said, "a couple of years ago. She was on the arm, rather pointedly, of a short dark man with crooked teeth."

"Really?" Jo said. "Where?"

"Would you believe Bomarzo?"

"When you were in Italy on that buying trip? There's nothing to buy at Bomarzo."

"I don't pretend to work all the time when I'm away," Frankie said.

Keyes wondered if the two shop owners weren't suffering from the end-of-the-season blues. It wasn't only actors who came down with that malady when autumn came around. The whole town tended to get a little crazy.

Frankie shrugged, then frowned and finished her drink, which seemed to contain plain fruit juice.

"Anyway," she went on, in a voice with the sound of ground glass in it, "despite my Venetian trews, Io pretended not to see me."

"Good for her," Julia said. "I mean, for leaving Pavel. He's a horrid old creature. Girls half his age!"

"More like a third," Jo said.

"'Maidens, like moths,'" Keyes quoted in the hope of finding a way into the conversation so he could ask about Brocken, "'are ever caught by the glare'..."

The three women looked at him as if he had tapioca for brains.

"What?" they said. Then they went back to the unfortunate Pavel.

"It's disgusting," Julia said. "You'd think he'd have learned by now..."

"At Pavel's age," said Sandra, who materialized suddenly on the edge of their group, Grace in her shadow. "There may be nothing left to learn, except what's taught by youth."

"Hello, Sandra," Keyes said. "I'm still looking for George Brocken."

"Are you, love? That's very tiresome for you, because he's left already."

"Are you sure? Hobie said..."

"Well, if he's still here," Sandra said as she turned grandly away, "I certainly haven't noticed him recently."

Keyes smiled wistfully and watched her go. Of course she hasn't noticed him, he told himself. She can't see anybody at parties except men she wants to flirt with, usually young men.

The band, approaching the end of a set, played at an ever more feverish pitch and rose to ever more thunderous loudness. Betty appeared before Keyes with a real berserker's look in her eye.

"Afar the contadina's song is heard," she bellowed above the roar of many massed guitars. "Rude but made sweet by distance!"

"Contadin-*o*, I believe," Keyes corrected at the top of his lungs.

"Bugger off!" Betty screamed, and veered away. Keyes hoped she was going home to bed, but he knew that would not be the case.

And suddenly there was silence, or what seemed like silence to Keyes after the effects of the band's finale. All about him he could suddenly hear conversation. Because of the music it too was turned up– everybody was speaking *fortissimo*; everybody was also too drunk to nôtice or care.

"In the morning sometimes," a tall woman from Communications confided to a small woman from Accommodations, "he still manages..."

"I'm not fond of hearing about marital difficulties."

"Oh, the wearisome irruminations!" The tall woman was a foreigner, Romanian, Keyes guessed, with a curious way of expressing herself in English. It seemed to him entirely appropriate that she was in the Communications department, the theatre world being as it was.

"Especially in the evening," the small woman said. "It puts me too much in mind of my own disappointments."

"And you've never tried turning to someone else?"

"I won't say never. I so much yearn to be want..." Her voice trailed off as she went away with her friend.

"Did she say want–*ed*?" Keyes wondered aloud.

"Want–*on*," said Hobart Porliss, who was once again on hand, "was what I heard."

"Did you? I was sure..."

"Doesn't pay to be sure about things– you'll only be disappointed."

"Hobie," Keyes said. "I've been wondering... why exactly were you out on the deck during the show the other night, when we found Wales?"

"Why were *you*?"

"Cigarette."

"Filthy habit– you should quit," Porliss said. "Actually, I was looking for that truly awful bust of Shakespeare that was lying beside Alan. An iron insult against the Bard, that statue– I think, subconsciously, I misplaced it on purpose. I'm glad it turned up... George gave it to me, and I wouldn't offend George for the world."

"And a bust of Shakespeare can be wonderful company," Keyes observed.

"Perhaps its just as well the police kept it, then; there's a lot to be said for the solitary life."

"Is there?"

"Even for masturbation. Your hand won't whine, nor will it look up in the middle of everything and say 'I think I'm falling in love with you.'"

Keyes laughed. At the moment he liked the portly director, despite himself. "I wouldn't know."

"What a fraud you are, Keyes!"

"Not really," Keyes said, defending himself. "It's just that I don't always speak quite from the heart."

"Unlike the rest of us," Porliss said, wheeling about and off, "so unlike the rest of us..."

Keyes found a post to lean against on the outskirts of a small group where O'Reilly was telling a story, in the spirit of the evening, about Alan Wales to Amalie Brown, the young actress playing Miranda in *The Tempest*. Damian Pace listened with a grimace on his swarthy face, remembering only too well the production of *Richard III* in which the incident occurred.

"This show was a real pig to begin with, very badly directed," O'Reilly said, with a wicked side glance toward Ms. Brown's escort, an intense assistant director. "I had nothing to do but stand onstage and look impressive. Anyway, Wales and I had a bet as to which of us could make the other one corpse first– "

"Corpse?" asked Amalie, wrinkling her turned-up nose. This was her first year at Stratford, and, although she had an undeniable talent, she was very conscious of the things she did not know, and strove to learn them.

O'Reilly, happy to instruct the young, explained: "Corpsing, wench, means laughing out loud onstage when you're not supposed to... it's great fun when you can get someone else to do it."

"Really, Seamus," the assistant said. "Laughing in the middle of a show is very poor form– you shouldn't be teaching Amalie your bad habits. Directors have enough trouble."

"When they're young, as you are, yes I suppose they do," O'Reilly said, miffed at having his story interrupted. "As I was saying, we had this bet on, and neither of us had managed to win. Then, one night near the end of the run, I was staring off into the wings, and there was Alan..." he trailed off, pausing to take a long sip of his whisky, "... with his pants down, mooning me; he had a lit cigar– "

"But no one's allowed to smoke backstage!" Amalie interrupted, obviously shocked at such a transgression. O'Reilly glared at her.

"The cigar was shoved up his arse!" he said with gleeful malice.

Damian Pace shook his head ruefully. Miss Brown flushed, sputtered, and nearly choked on the beer she had the misfortune to drink at that moment.

"Oh, my God!" she said when she recovered. "Alan Wales won the bet then?"

"Certainly not!" O'Reilly said. "*I* am a professional. Damian was standing next to me, so I nudged him and whispered 'Look at that asshole in the wings.' Poor *Damian* corpsed and almost forgot his next lines. The director gave him a terrific lecture, and Alan caught hell from stage-management. It was a wonderful night."

A solemn shadow passed over O'Reilly's face. "I suppose I've won that bet, after all..."

"Why is that?" asked the innocent actress.

"Alan has certainly corpsed now," O'Reilly answered quietly.

Amalie Brown excused herself to find a secluded corner, where she sat for the rest of the night, a large glass of beer in each hand. Keyes assumed she was pondering her future with this particular crew of people.

Later in the evening, Keyes heard Sandra's voice from the stage, alternating with O'Reilly's, then recognized with pleasure a project that the two actors were developing, and had talked about previewing. It was a two-hander with the working title of *Cain and Eve*, dramatizing excerpts from the works of Lord Byron, specifically exchanges between male and female characters.

O'Reilly might have been born to bring Byron and his words to life, while Sandra's deft and delicate handling of the various women at times rendered Keyes breathless with awe, reminding him of how truly gifted she was, and of other things about her.

SANDRA

My office is
Henceforth to dry up tears, not to shed them;
But yet, of all who mourn, none mourn like me,
Not only for myself, but him who slew thee.
Now, Cain! I will divide thy burden with thee.

O'REILLY

Eastward from Eden will we make our way;
'Tis the most desolate, and suits my steps.

SANDRA

Lead! Thou shalt be my guide, and may our God
Be thine! Now let us carry forth our children.

O'REILLY

And he who lieth there was childless. I
Have dried the fountain of a gentle race,
Which might have temper'd this stern blood of mine,
Uniting with our children Abel's offspring!
O Abel!

SANDRA

Peace be with him!

O'REILLY

But with me!

This was well-received by the crowd, even though by the end O'Reilly was beginning to show signs of over-indulgence. A line of text from some other long-lost triumph slipped into his speech, and this he managed to spoonerize. The result was his loud demand of Sandra: "What fuel crate has brought you here?"

The audience howled with laughter and applauded enthusiastically. Sandra, to Keyes' surprise, slammed her notebook shut and stalked away in anger. Normally, she would simply have shot back some quick and witty response, in character and without missing a beat. Keyes supposed her to be much more upset than she would ever let on in public over the death of Wales. O'Reilly bowed uncertainly, and made his exit as well. He looked as if he had no idea what had just happened.

Finally Keyes caught sight of George Brocken, who had in fact been present all along, if elusive. He was in a far corner of the room, well away from the bar, and away from the stage too. Propped against a wall with a glass in his hand, he was watching the crowd as it milled back and forth before him. Somehow he seemed out of context, like a crow among pigeons.

"Mr. Brocken," Keyes said. "Can I buy you a drink?"

Brocken looked at him. There was no expression in his eyes, not even curiosity.

"I have a drink," he said. "Besides, my mother taught me not to drink with strangers."

"I'm Claude Keyes. I was in the company years ago. You were around then, too, but I didn't work in any of the shows you designed."

"Are you the writer Hobie told me about?"

"I write. What did he tell you about me?"

"Just gossip," Brocken said, smiling ever so slightly.

"What sort of gossip?"

Brocken looked back at the milling crowd. "I can't remember. Something about you and Sandra, I think. I don't pay much attention to Hobart, especially when he's gossiping."

"That's very shrewd of you," Keyes said.

"Oh, I'm nothing if not shrewd." He turned again to Keyes and his eyes suggested that he was indeed very shrewd. "Did you want something? Or are you like Hobart... just here to gossip?"

"As a matter of fact, I do want something... or rather I want to talk to you about something."

Brocken waited. His gaze did not shift or change in character. It was intensely shrewd.

"I was looking at some of your drawings this afternoon," Keyes continued.

"Is that so? Did you like them?"

Keyes hadn't really thought about the drawings that way. He had been too astonished at their content, or at least by the content of one of them to bother about their style. Certainly he didn't like them as well as he liked the Kirkpatricks, or the Heeleys...

"They are very... deft," he said.

Brocken barked a short laugh. "As much as that? What do you really want, Mr. Keyes?"

"It's difficult to say. It was the *Macbeth* designs I saw."

Brocken nodded. "At Smoke and Mirrors. Charming women. Hobart says they're lovers."

"Are they?"

"No. Hobie thinks everybody is gay because he is. Both of them have been married and have children."

"All the more reason perhaps," Keyes speculated.

"That's as may be, but I have personal and incontrovertible evidence otherwise..."

Keyes was not deaf to the note of masculine pride which accompanied Brocken's statement.

"...well, this is a theatre party after all," Keyes muttered.

"Are you perhaps planning a book about my sex life, Mr. Keyes?"

"No... what I've really been trying to get around to is—Alan Wales."

Keyes felt a new rigidity in the man standing beside him. It was almost as if some internal drill sergeant had suddenly called Brocken to attention.

"What about Alan Wales?" the designer said carefully.

"It was your drawing of him that made me want to talk to you."

"I see. And not just because you admired its brilliant technique."

"No," Keyes admitted. "It was the pose. I found Wales, you know... after his death."

"Ah, so you're the one. I didn't remember the name. Not very pleasant stumbling on a corpse... or 'corse,' as the Bard might say."

"It made me sick," Keyes said, "literally."

"Well?"

"Well what?"

"What are you trying to tell me?" Brocken said in an exasperated voice.

"The body..." Keyes paused. Even mentioning it made him a bit queasy. "The pose, the position of it, the gesture– it was exactly like your drawing."

"You're very observant," Brocken said quietly. "I'm not used to such observation among my critics or admirers. People *have* commented on Damian's clothes..."

"Brave Macbeth."

"And Sandra's frocks, and Seamus' robe, but Alan's soldier suit? Not a word has been said about that."

"Until now," Keyes said.

Brocken looked away and took a couple of beats before he spoke.

"As you say," he replied, "until now. A pity, too, because I'm quite proud of that costume. I worked on it every bit as hard as I worked on the principals. He's Act I, Scene 2... right after the witches. The bloody man, as Duncan calls him, announces the wars, the struggle, the violence that is to follow."

"Mr. Brocken, I– "

"Call me George. Anybody with an eye as sharp as yours should call me George."

For the first time since their interview had begun, Keyes saw that Brocken was drunk. This didn't surprise him; everyone else was also drunk. What surprised him was how little Brocken showed it.

"Yes... well then, George, it occurred to me–"

Brocken interrupted. "It occurred to you that you were not the 'first one' to find the body after all."

"Something like that. He– Alan Wales– was so like your drawing. He can't have fallen that way by accident, can he?"

"Have you told anyone about this?"

Keyes shook his head. "For some reason I wanted to talk to you before..."

"Before what?"

"Before I went to the police, I guess."

"What do you suppose they will make of it?"

"No idea," Keyes admitted.

"I've a hunch they won't understand it very well," Brocken said quietly. Then he added: "Oh, they'll understand as much as you do... as much as you do at this moment, I mean."

"That you were there before me... that you..."

"I didn't kill him, so don't bother to suggest that. I did get to him before you did, and I did... move things about a little."

"Things!"

"Him, then. I couldn't bear seeing it all wrong."

"It!?"

"The costume. Not once had that silly twit Wales managed to get into it properly. I dressed him myself the week before we opened, Grace took a crack at instructing him, and always by the time he went on, he had it all wrong again. The baldrick..." Brocken broke off and rubbed his eyes as if to rid himself of the fatal vision of a baldrick badly worn.

Keyes said nothing, but wished he had another drink.

"I knew there would be photographs, you see... of the corpse. There always are. Bad enough to have him appear that way out there on the wet pavement, but in the newspapers! That costume was all right. It was even quite successful, but Wales made it look terrible. And by getting himself killed, he made it look even worse. I had to do something about it."

"That's craziness, George," Keyes said.

"Is it?" Brocken replied brightly. "It may be, but it is, nevertheless, what I do. It is my job to get the costumes right."

"Onstage, yes, but..."

Brocken wasn't listening now, not to Keyes anyway.

"I forgot about the drawing at Smoke and Mirrors," he said. "They've had it for months. The cutters worked from a later version."

Keyes started to say something, then stopped himself.

Brocken looked at him and smiled as broadly as his tight features would allow. "I really am flattered, you know. What an eye you have!"

"Flattered!"

"So much of a designer's work goes unnoticed. It's very discouraging at times."

"But George, the police..."

"Oh, them. They'll never find the drawing. Even if they did, they wouldn't see what it meant. Jo at Smoke and Mirrors has an excellent eye; so has Frankie– and *they* haven't noticed."

"They didn't see the corpse," Keyes said grimly.

"Of course they did. Everybody did. The photographs were in all the papers, as I knew they would be, the less gory ones, anyway. You were the only one with the intelligence and the... the connoisseurship to make the connection. I'm very impressed."

"He did look more... more dramatic than I've heard he ever was onstage," Keyes murmured.

"You see?" Brocken crowed. "He was wearing his costume properly. That's why he looked 'dramatic.'"

"But someone must be told about all this."

"Who? The police?" Brocken asked. "Why should they know? I moved things about a little. I made some alterations, aesthetic adjustments. I made Alan Wales look better for the photographers. That's all."

"You made yourself look better, too... better as a designer anyway."

"Not better than I am," Brocken said. "I just set matters right. I had nothing to do with the silly twit's death."

"I wish you'd stop calling him that." Keyes said. "Nothing?"

"Absolutely nothing."

"What were you doing out there in the first place?"

Brocken frowned. "You *are* tenacious. Hobie was terribly upset because he'd misplaced a gift I'd given him. He gets very wrought-up about little things, and he is my friend, so I was out there looking for it."

"Well, you found it... the Shakespeare thing."

"That I did."

"So why didn't you take it? Certainly not because you were worried about tampering with evidence..."

Brocken shrugged. "Symmetry, I suppose. It looked to me like Shakespeare was deep in conversation with Wales. Why disturb them?"

Somehow Keyes knew that Brocken was telling the truth.

"I think I'm going to need another drink," Keyes said.

"I shouldn't be a bit surprised," Brocken said sympathetically. "And you know, I think I need one, too."

He took Keyes' arm and led him through the crowd toward the bar.

"We should have lunch together some time," he said. "Most people in the theatre are blind, don't see anything except what looks back at them from the mirror. But you—*you* have an eye!"

After a brief drink with Brocken, Keyes decided to make his escape. It was about 1:30 a.m., and the affair was hitting its full stride. There was little talk about Wales, or the late Ricardo, or of anything else of any consequence. There was now other business afoot, that of courting serious derangement of the senses and of finding companionship for the long night's journey into morning. Neither of these activities currently interested Keyes, and so he slipped out without anyone being the wiser.

The collapse of his theory concerning Brocken had not cured him of the desire to know what had really happened. If anything, his curiosity was now keener.

He walked past Dead Swan Isle, pausing there once more, this time to look up at the clear night sky, in time to see a star detach itself from its fellows and fall dying toward the horizon. The falling star triggered a series of impressions similar to those which had led him to suspect Brocken. He was perhaps not so quick to trust his impressions this time, but still...

A love-hate scene played before the opening curtain of *Macbeth*... tales of abuse... sequins... lost Shakespeares... and Kiri Ellison.

He quickened his pace, hoping to reach The Gilded Lily before it shut its doors for the night.

(4:3) The Gilded Lily

The Lily had not quite folded its ragged petals, although the serving of alcohol had officially ceased an hour earlier. Keyes had never been inside the place at such a late hour, or on a Saturday night. The bar bore even less resemblance to a haven of entertainment and good fellowship than it usually did.

A patron was lowered over his table, eyes closed and snoring heavily. Two bald men, one whose pate was bisected by a ragged scar, faced each other over the billiards table, holding their cues like pikestaffs as they disputed the score. A man in an expensive three-piece suit sat before the empty stage, hands folded in his lap, staring up as if awaiting a vision. Three bikers groped a female member of their club beneath the Daily Special sign.

As Keyes made his way through, his shoes occasionally stuck to the floor, grasped by spilt liquor and other nameless fluids. Raw guitars and drums pummelled the thick clouds of smoke that hung low beneath ineffectual ceiling fans.

Keyes' first impulse was to make a straight line for the exit door, but then he saw Kiri Ellison standing by the bar, in conversation or argument with the bartender, who in all probability was the proprietor as well. The bartender had a wad of bills clutched tightly in his fist, no doubt the subject of his interchange with Kiri.

At last the man peeled some bills from the roll and thrust them at Kiri with poor grace. There was something very strange about the tableau, and Keyes realized what it was after a moment's reflection: although the bartender was a hulking brute of a man whose knuckles probably scraped the floor when he walked, the diminutive Kiri seemed somehow to be the larger of the two, no mean feat– she was clad only in the tiniest of G-strings and a small mask which suggested the visage of a bird.

Of prey? Keyes wondered.

Just as Keyes reached Kiri, the music ended abruptly and harsh fluorescent lights came up full, revealing with brutal honesty the disrepair and neglect beneath the peeling gilding of The Lily and its patrons. But Kiri was still beautiful, he saw, perhaps the only thing of beauty in this abysmal place.

Keyes had no idea what to say to this girl, how to voice his suspicions, which admittedly had their roots only in slim circumstance, dreams, and guesswork. Approaching George Brocken had been relatively simple, since they had the theatre as common background. Keyes knew nothing about Kiri's life other than hearsay, gossip, and their one brief conversation outside The Bells. He had, however, concluded one thing about her from that meeting: that she was a blunt, straightforward person; she would probably respond best to the same traits in others. Or so he hoped.

"Miss Ellison?" he said. She was standing alone now, counting the money.

She removed her bird mask, and tucked the bills in the G-string.

"You again... slumming?" she asked, her tone neutral and disinterested.

Keyes took a deep breath, then plunged forward.

"No. I need to talk to you, in private. I have reason to think that you killed Alan Wales..."

Keyes was more or less prepared for violence, tears, loud denials, and so forth, but not for the sad calmness of her reply:

"I figured somebody would come to that conclusion sooner or later," Kiri said. "I'll grab some clothes. Meet me outside in a couple of minutes and we can get this over with."

(4:4) Big Bill's, a doughnut shop

Kiri came out a side door of The Lily, wearing her jeans and leather jacket. "Come on," she said, leading him across the street to Big Bill's, an all-night doughnut franchise. It was empty, except for a gum-chewing teenaged girl at the counter, who poured two mugs of coffee as soon as she saw Kiri and Keyes enter. They sat at a table near a window looking out on an intersection. On the other three corners, there were churches.

"Well?" Kiri said. "What do you think you know?"

Keyes told her of witnessing the rendezvous with Wales before the performance of *Macbeth*, and of the sequins he had found beside the body; he explained what he knew of how badly she had been treated by Wales. He did not tell her of his dream.

"I know none of this is solid evidence," he concluded, "but I had a feeling that you were involved, somehow– "

"Are you going to the police?" she demanded.

Keyes sipped at his coffee.

"No," he said at last. "I don't think so. I just want to know what happened. I feel like I've been reading a book that somebody tore the last page out of. I want to find that last page."

"Well, I haven't got it," Kiri said. "When you saw Alan and me, we were having a fight, as usual, but then he had to go to work, so he told me to meet him later under that well thing. We'd done it before. I wasn't going to go, but I've never been able to stay mad at him. When I got there, he wanted... he liked..." She paused, then stared at Keyes defiantly, as if challenging him to be shocked. "He liked blow-jobs in public places. But this time, he kept glancing up that well, as if he were expecting somebody to be there."

Keyes interrupted.

"It seems to me he treated you pretty badly... Why did you put up with it?"

"Alan and I went to school together. We're both from St. Marys, you know. He was the first guy I ever slept with. And when he came back here, he told me he'd help me get into acting school, or something like that. This dancing job pays well enough, so I decided to take it until Alan set something up for me in the theatre. Course, he never even took me to a play, but I was in love with him, no matter what he did. I don't expect you to understand that..."

Keyes thought of Sandra, and his own history with her.

"I think I do," he said softly.

"Then I heard footsteps, and a woman's voice– she said 'Alan, you bastard,' or something like that."

Kiri stopped talking, and stared out the window for a moment, toward the churches.

"I raised my head, but all I could see was Alan," she continued. "I didn't want anything to do with a scene like that. I just took off. I ran down to the island. It's where I like to go to get my head together. And that's it, the whole story. I didn't kill him. Maybe I should have. He was a bastard, and I can do better. But I didn't, and I have no intention of telling the cops about that woman, whoever she was– I guess I'm sorry Alan's dead... but maybe she did us all a favour."

"You seemed to care when I saw you outside in the rain the other day," Keyes reminded her.

"Maybe I've had time to think," Kiri said, sadly.

Keyes reached into his jacket for cigarettes. The sequins had attached themselves to the package. He plucked them off, one by one, and handed them to her.

"I believe you," he said. "I guess I'll just keep looking for that last page. You really didn't get a glimpse of the woman?"

Kiri shook her head.

As a detective, I make a great sculptor, Keyes thought, standing up.

"I'm sorry to have bothered you, Miss Ellison, and I hope you're not offended by my suspicions."

"I guess I should thank you for letting me explain my side of it. Some people wouldn't have taken the time. I think... you must have loved somebody once, too."

"I guess I must have," Keyes said. Then, for no reason he could put his finger on, Keyes added "May I walk you home, Miss Ellison?"

An expression crossed her face that made her look very young and very innocent for a moment, until a frown knitted her thick brows, perhaps as she wondered what the catch was, since in her life up until now, there probably *always* was a catch to kindness, usually a sexual one. In this case, however, she must have decided otherwise.

"Thank you," she said. "That would be nice. I don't live far."

They made a strange duo as they walked unhurriedly to a neighbourhood near the railroad tracks, but certainly no stranger than many of the couples in the clash of cultures that inhabit Stratford during its warm dramatic summers, and cool moody autumns.

(4:5) Sunday, Bloody Sunday, Part I

Keyes felt terrible the next day. He was so unwell that he did not get up. Stratford, he thought as he lay in his hired bed, was too much for him. He could no longer deal with the pace that Stratfordians maintained, at least the Stratfordians of his acquaintance.

He had slowed his drinking down enormously since he left the stage. His life as a writer was tame compared to the life most actors led until age or children slowed them down. Keyes had almost forgotten about the burden of left-over energy that so many actors carried with them into the pub after the last lines were spoken and the last bit of applause had faded away. He had forgotten the passion of it all, and the raging thirsts.

It had not been his intention when he returned to Stratford to try to get back into the magical world he had known there once upon a time. He didn't want to keep up with his theatrical friends. Even in his play-acting years he had never been able to keep up with many of them, especially the mighty O'Reilly. Sandra, too, had frequently drunk him under the boards. Her appetites generally were grander than his, more urgent, more sweeping. Even Betty had a capacity for drink and perhaps for life that made Keyes feel, at least on this hangover morning, that he was only a frail creature, a monkish introvert.

I can't even get any writing done in this circus, he thought. He had not completed a single paragraph on the life and times of Seamus O'Reilly during the past week, which, after all, was the main purpose of his visit to Stratford. He supposed he could plead murder as an extenuating circumstance to whatever court passes judgement on writers who do not write.

He groaned and heaped pillows over his head. In the distance he heard a church bell, and then another. That distance was not distant enough. Keyes heard the bells, and felt them as well— painfully, as if the bronze clappers were inside his own head.

Stratford's real people, as opposed to its Theatre People, were behaving much as real people throughout North America behave on Sunday morning. Some were in church, on their way to church, or on their way home from church. Many more were worshipping at home before their television screens. These people worshipped strange and exotic gods: evangelical freaks, wise-cracking rabbits, athletes struggling with one another like mating mastodons, gabby matrons with flour-dusted forearms, demonic super machines— automobiles, trucks, boats, motorcycles, and even less logical devices.

A few people were out of doors. Some of these jogged. Others dreamily walked their dogs, or children, or both.

The coffee shops were busy as they always were on the morning after a theatre party. Relationships had dissolved or exploded during the double wake the night before, and subsequently new ones had been established. Some of the survivors of this great game of musical beds looked remarkably fit; others were less fortunate, and looked desperate, as if they knew terrible mistakes had been made. Nobody was very pretty. They had been pretty the night before, but on this

Morning After they relaxed in their stubbly beards and ratty hair doing nothing to disguise bleary eyes, lined and pouched faces, general grubbiness. They wore anything but what the pious world would consider "Sunday clothes." They celebrated no cult on Sunday morning. Their rituals had been performed on Saturday night, first in the theatre, then on the dance floor, then in their several beds. They were the Bacchae, or what was left of them.

There was another reason why Keyes chose not to get up, a reason more difficult and more solemn than having a hangover. He had a new suspicion as to who had killed Alan Wales, had suspected it even when he went to bed the night before, but had not allowed himself to admit it.

It was because of this inadmissible knowledge that he had spent Saturday afternoon and some of Saturday night playing the part of the first of all detectives, Poe's Auguste Dupin. He didn't want to accept what his instinct had tried to tell him from the beginning. He would have liked to find another murderer for Alan Wales.

Unfair as it was of him, he would have preferred to convince himself that George Brocken was the killer. He didn't know Brocken or particularly care for him, so he had imagined him in the role easily. But Brocken turned out to be only a meddler, and an artist of the theatre who valued effect above all else.

Keyes had never seriously suspected Kiri, either. She was too obviously Wales' victim, and as he had found out, had been too much in love with him. Playing detective with her was largely the fault of her sequins, or her stars, as he preferred to think of them. No one with imagination could ignore the discovery of so many small silver stars in such ominous, or at least mysterious, places. And by investigating Kiri he had managed to avoid for a few more hours his inevitable confrontation with the real murderer.

It was already evening when Keyes finally got himself going. Betty's house was silent, and seemed empty. Most of the people who came to Stratford for Shakespeare were on their way home now. There were occasional performances on Sunday evening, but the theatres were closed on Mondays. Betty's other guests, in any case, seemed to have fled.

"Betty," Keyes called tentatively in the direction of the kitchen, "are you in there?"

Evidently she was not, so Keyes went in and helped himself to his landlady's tea, minus her personal additives. He took the tea to the second floor balcony down the hall from his room, and sat sipping and smoking, screened from passersby on the street below by the leaves of the giant elm tree on the front lawn. The evening was mild and pleasantly calm. With the majority of the tourists gone, the stench of exhaust fumes had diminished and the carbon monoxide level was down.

He felt better when he had drunk a cup of black Ceylon, and better still after three of them. He started a fourth, but realized that another cup of tea would, as his mother always said, leave his back teeth floating, and so he did not finish it.

"Why is it so difficult to be moderate in this town?" he grumbled at himself.

At last, he dressed and got himself in motion. As he walked along the riverbank, Keyes smelled flowers, or imagined that he did– the last of the roses, he supposed. He also smelled decay, the sweet odour of rotting leaves.

He crossed the river on the dam that contained Lake Victoria, then climbed the hill beyond it to the old house where Sandra lived. There were no lights burning in it, but that, he knew, didn't mean that Sandra wasn't home. She liked the twilight and often sat by her window looking out into it.

"*L'heure bleue*," she had often called it in her precise but un-French French. "It's my favourite time of day."

Keyes climbed the steps to the front door. It stood a bit ajar.

Again he called out for somebody, as earlier he had called out for Betty.

"Hello," he said. "Is anyone home?"

His voice echoed up the staircase, or some voice did, sounding almost too sepulchral to Keyes to be his own.

Something creaked a storey above him, then the house was silent again.

"Hello up there," he called again. "Sandra, it's me. It's Claude."

Again there was no reply. Even so Keyes sensed that he was not alone. He put his hand on the bannister and started to climb in the darkness. The gentle spiral of the staircase made this easy enough even with so little light.

On the second floor landing something loomed up before him, loomed so abruptly that he almost lost his footing.

"What do you want?" a shrill voice shrieked. "Sandra's not here."

The voice belonged to Grace Lockhardt. Keyes recognized it, but only barely. He had never heard it like this before, so shrill and overwrought, almost hysterical.

"I'm sorry, Grace," he said as calmly as he could. After the fright Grace's apparition had given him, he was feeling a bit unsteady. "Aren't the lights working?"

"She's not here. Go away."

Keyes ran his hand along the wall, found a light switch, and pushed it. A sickly glimmer from a chandelier on the floor below transformed the darkness into still another version of twilight. Grace shrank back into the shadows of the second storey hall. She was dressed in some sort of wrapper. Her hair was all about her face, a face streaked by tears. Her eyes were wide and ferocious. Keyes had seen cornered animals with that look in their eyes– cats and even smaller creatures. He knew better than to go any closer to her.

"I'll scream," Grace said in a strangled voice.

"I'm sorry, Grace. I just wanted to speak to Sandra. Can you tell me where she is?"

At last the frightened woman seemed to recognize Keyes. She straightened up and pawed her hair away from her face.

"Oh, it's you," she mumbled. "I thought..."

"What did you think?"

"I've been asleep... your voice; I thought you were Alan."

"No, Grace, not Alan. Just Claude. Are you all right?"

"I suppose so... no– I'm frightened."

"Frightened of what? Wales is dead."

Grace shook her head desperately, then struggled again with her matted hair.

"It's not that," she said.

"What, then?"

"Sandra... she didn't come home last night."

There was raw anguish in the woman's voice, in her face, in the way she held her hands and her body.

"But you were together at the party..." Keyes began.

"She sent me home... in a cab... said she'd be along soon. I waited all night."

Grace stopped, gasping for air, then burst again into tears.

"I'm so afraid," she groaned, as Keyes put his arm around her and led her into her apartment.

"What you need is a cup of tea," he said. "I'll make some."

Keyes did so, then finally succeeded in calming Grace down by promising to go off in search of Sandra.

"But where could she be?" Grace wailed as he was closing the door to her apartment behind him.

A good question, Keyes thought. Stratford was not a big town but it did have many hiding places, at least enough to obscure the many romances of its theatrical population, its tourists, who did not always arrive in legally married couples, and its randier locals.

"Sandra might be anywhere," Keyes confided to a passing cat, as he left the house.

Then it occurred to him that she might even have left town. Trains ran to Toronto and all the Canadian cities beyond. There was a daily train south, which terminated in Chicago. There were buses, and taxi-cabs, and airport limousines, and planes that could be chartered out of the small private airport...

In the end, however, Keyes did not think that Sandra would run away. She had a contract, after all, and scheduled performances in the days to come. She was too loyal to her vocation and to the actors she worked with to walk out on a production. She was a trouper.

Again he crossed the river by the dam. The Avon's waters at that point were very deep, deep enough to hide a body, surely, or several of them. There had been a case only a few seasons earlier– a suicide, or a murder perhaps... There had never been any very satisfactory explanations for that grim event.

"Not Sandra," Keyes told himself. "She gets angry, furious, but she's not a candidate for the Slough of Despond. She's still in Stratford... somewhere."

(4:6) Sunday, Bloody Sunday, Part II

Inevitably perhaps, he went to the Festival theatre. There was no performance that evening. The big building was nearly deserted, slumbering. Even so, there were lights at the stage entrance, and a man on duty there. He was knitting. He had always been knitting in those distant days when Keyes had first known him.

"Hello, Ivor," Keyes said. "What are you making now?"

Ivor looked up, squinted, then smiled as he recognized Keyes.

"Evening, Claude," he said. "Socks for the Red Cross. They always need them."

Keyes mumbled something about supposing that they always did.

"You're probably looking for Miss Edel," the old man went on.

"I probably am," Keyes agreed. "Has she been here?"

Ivor nodded. "All afternoon. She said she wanted to run some lines. Hasn't even been out to eat."

"I thought maybe she'd go out for something with me."

"You never give up, do you? Still carrying a torch."

"Can't help it, Ivor."

"Oh, I understand, all right... It wouldn't be easy to get over a woman like that, I don't imagine."

Keyes said nothing. He had thought his torch-light safely hidden under a bushel. But if Ivor knew he was in love with

Sandra, then everybody in the company probably knew as well.

"Want me to call her down?" the guard asked.

"No. I'll go up. Even if she agrees to dinner, it'll take her a while to get ready."

Ivor laughed. "She's always on, isn't she, Claude?"

"Always," Keyes agreed.

Sandra was not in her dressing room, and for a moment Keyes thought that Ivor might have made a mistake about her presence in the theatre. She might, he supposed, have left without being seen by Ivor.

He was about to go back downstairs when he heard a voice, only barely. But, faint as it was, he knew the voice was Sandra's. Like a dog homing on a familiar call, he followed the sound of her.

Sandra was downstage centre, on the great thrust-stage that jutted away from the proscenium out into the awesomely dark and empty house. There was no illumination for her except a work light, raw and harsh. She was wearing rehearsal clothes: a full black skirt over a black leotard, soft little boots, also black. She had some sort of a tropical shawl– a serape of many colours– bundled about her torso. Her hair was bound up piratically by still more black. Keyes thought her very beautiful.

In spite of what Ivor had promised, Sandra was not merely running lines. She was performing as if to a full house, and one that had in it somewhere not only royalty but a dozen of the world's greatest producers.

"...the smell of blood still..." Keyes heard her say in the moment before she perceived him approaching from the shadowy wings.

"Hello, Claude," she said. She was making nervous motions with her hands, a combination of her ring-twisting mannerism and of the guilty hand-washing from her performance of Lady Macbeth's sleepwalking scene.

"I went to your flat. Grace is a mess."

"Poor Grace. I just couldn't deal with her last night. I couldn't deal with anybody..."

"You've been here all that time?"

Sandra nodded. "I slept in my dressing room... but I didn't sleep."

Keyes put his hand out to her, but she turned and crossed to the far side of the stage.

"I'd rather not be touched," she said. "Don't take it personally."

He laughed, briefly and without humour.

"It's my great flaw," he said. "I can't help taking things personally."

"Maybe that's why you weren't a very good actor," Sandra said. There was a touch of tenderness in her voice, but only a touch.

"Maybe," Keyes said. "You can talk to me, you know."

Sandra looked at him oddly. "I am talking to you."

"I mean about Alan."

"What about Alan...?" She paused, then went on. "I see. About the murder, you mean."

"Is there anything else to talk about on a night like this?"

"Perhaps not. Have you figured it out, then?"

Keyes hesitated. Something about her tone made him unsure of himself; she had always had a talent for making him feel insecure.

"You know who killed him?" Sandra continued, pressing him now, defying him, almost.

"I think I do."

"And exactly what do you think?"

"I've seen you play Vittoria Corombona, Sandra," Keyes said.

"Vittoria?..."

"Vittoria could have done it, and the part of you that is Vittoria... don't ask me to make sense of it. I can't."

Sandra turned slowly and looked into the phantom audience.

"Yes," she said solemnly. "Vittoria could have done it. But Claude, I'm not Vittoria, except when I'm playing her onstage. Another of the reasons you weren't a very good actor, you know, is that you could never keep straight what was stage and what was life."

Keyes said nothing to this, but as usual he had to admit that Sandra's judgement of him was sound. Illusion? Reality? He had often been muddled by the distinction. Never, perhaps, more than now.

"No, Claude, I didn't kill Alan."

He accepted it at once, absolutely.

"I apologize, then," he said. He meant it.

"But I know who did..."

Then, still gazing out into the house, Sandra told him about it, or told that invisible audience. An audience was the only judge, the only jury, that she had ever respected, and an audience, or the symbol of one, was what she now addressed.

Keyes listened, as he had always done, and wondered whether he would or should applaud this performance when Sandra had done with it.

She told about her romance with Wales, about the passion, the violence, the hatefully delicious humiliations. She told Keyes that her lover had come to her dressing room that night, to make love to her, or, as he more precisely put it, to "have sex with her."

"I probably would have," she said, "if there had been only a bit more time, another few minutes."

She told him that Wales had whispered to her in the wings just before intermission, demanding to see her.

"I thought I knew exactly what he wanted," she said grimly. "And I was right, but he wanted it from that slut who strips."

Keyes thought about interrupting to explain that the "slut who strips" wasn't really a bad sort of a kid, but in the end he knew better than to try this.

"He also wanted to punish me," Sandra added.

"Punish you? For what?"

"For not giving him what he wanted when he asked for it."

And for being The Real Thing, Keyes thought. Frauds like Wales hated nothing so much as The Real Thing.

"He asked you to meet him on the Marquee deck," Keyes guessed.

Sandra nodded. "There was no one there when I went out. I whispered his name a time or two, then I heard something at the far end of the deck– a sort of scuffling sound."

"Down by that strange hole..."

"I went there– quietly, in case it was someone else."

"But it wasn't someone else," Keyes supplied.

Sandra took a deep breath, then let the air out very slowly. She was making those motions with her hands again, wringing them as she had been when Keyes found her on the stage. He was suddenly afraid for her, as Grace had said she was, afraid she might faint, or scream, or tear her hair out.

"Sandra..." he began.

But she wouldn't let him speak.

"It was Alan all right," she said, her voice grating with emotion, "and his whore. She was down on her knees in front of him, and she wasn't tying his shoes."

"You think he wanted you to see...?"

"I know he did." She paused. "He wanted to see how I'd react. I suppose he expected me to cry, or plead, or something."

"But you didn't."

"Of course I didn't, but I reacted, all right, and a bit more extravagantly than he probably expected. I went down the ramp, down the steps... I don't know how I didn't kill myself in that frock I was wearing."

Keyes couldn't help but laugh. He had seen Sandra angry and could imagine how awesome she must have been, in full costume and bearing down on Wales and Kiri– not much less awesome, he thought, than the Spanish Armada.

"The girl looked up from her work," Sandra went on. "She didn't say anything; I guess she'd been taught not to talk with her mouth full. Then she disappeared."

"And Alan?"

Sandra's great bosom heaved. "Alan... laughed at me."

"Alan lived dangerously," Keyes allowed.

"So I punched him in the mouth." She said it simply, as if that had been her only choice of action.

Again Keyes felt the impulse to laugh, and might have done so uproariously over the whole farcical scene Sandra was describing, had it not ended in such a macabre fashion.

Sandra held up her hand. "I hit him hard. Broke the stone in my ring."

"You broke a couple of his front teeth, too."

"I have rarely enjoyed anything so much."

Keyes thought for a moment. "But I still don't understand..."

Sandra refused to be rushed. She had become the principal speaker in this scene, and was playing it accordingly.

"He didn't laugh after that," she said. "He whined a little about his face. Then he grabbed me. I'd had enough by then, and besides, I had a scene to do."

"But he grabbed you."

"Tore my frock," Sandra said. "Ripped the shoulder..."

"You should have called for help."

"I should have, but I didn't, and then I couldn't– Alan started choking me."

Sandra put her hand to her throat and drew her collar down a little. The bruises she exposed were purplish and ugly.

"I think he was trying to kill me," she said, in a voice that betrayed something like strain, at last. "Perhaps he might have... if not for Grace."

"Grace?" Keyes remembered how distraught the dresser had been earlier in the evening.

"Yes. You know how she follows me about, hardly ever lets me out of her sight, especially during a show."

"Why didn't *she* get help?"

Sandra shrugged. "I don't know; I guess she thought she didn't have time."

"From the sound of it, she was probably right."

"Alan saw Grace, but Alan kept on throttling me. She tried to pull him off me, but he just called her a 'dirty bitch,' or something equally characteristic of Alan, and squeezed me harder. Grace grabbed at his belt... Alan let go of me. I fell over, and lay there trying to get my breath. When I got up again, Alan was flat on his back. Grace was standing over him with the knife in her hand."

"But for God's sakes, Sandra," Keyes said, "you should have told somebody. He *was* trying to kill you, after all."

"But we didn't. All I could think about was my next scene. I told Grace to get rid of the knife. She ran off, and I went back into the theatre."

"What did she do with it?" Keyes wondered.

"I don't know... threw it in the lake, I think."

Just like that, Keyes thought. Sandra said it so flatly, so easily, as if Grace had casually discarded a kleenex or a cigarette butt. He could see it only too well in his mind's eye—the terrified woman, thin and awkward, running with the bloody blade in her hand, then the sweeping movement of her arm as she rid herself of the evidence of her violence.

This image of Grace's gesture and of the weapon tumbling over and over through the wet night air hung frozen in Keyes' imagination; he remembered one of his dreams, and in that moment solved another of the Stratford mysteries.

"The swan," he said under his breath, "the poor swan..."

"What did you say?" Sandra said. Her voice was the voice of a child, a very weary, very frightened child.

"Nothing," Keyes said, "that matters."

"It's all so horrible," Sandra said. "Poor Grace..."

"You could still go to the police..." Keyes began, but he knew this bit of advice would not be taken. The scandal of such a confession might mean the end of Sandra's career. Neither she nor Grace would be able to live with a disaster like that.

For a little while they stayed where they were on the empty stage, with Sandra staring out into the empty house, and Keyes staring at Sandra.

Then she stook a step toward the apron. Her shawl slipped slowly from her shoulders and fell in a heap beside her. For a moment Keyes thought she was going to fall. He sprang forward, steadied her. This time she allowed herself to be touched.

"Do you suppose you could take me home, love?" she murmured. "I'm so terribly tired."

ACT FIVE

When the Hurly Burly's Done

O, Sisters Three,
Come, come to me,
With hands as pale as milk;
Lay them in gore,
Since you have shore
With shears his thread of silk...
– *A Midsummer Night's Dream*, Act V, Scene 1

(5:1) The Tempest

Keyes might have wept with joy, were he a weeping man. As it was, he settled for a smile which stretched from his left ear almost to the right ear of the woman in the neighbouring seat. For tonight he had struck gold.

Right from the start of the play, it was not his best friend Seamus dressed up in borrowed identity striding about on the stage; it was Prospero, the wronged Duke of Milan, heavy with dignity and aflame with rough magic. Beside the wizard was no giddy ingenue, but a fresh-faced and innocently nubile Miranda, moon-eyed at the wondrous alien creatures who had appeared on her island.

Everything that could possibly go right with the Festival's closing production had done so, and Claude Keyes was remembering what had first brought him into this perpetually chaotic and often dangerous world so many years ago. If anything could have tempted him back into the heaven and hell that was the profession of acting, this *Tempest* was it.

But the past is past, he thought happily, and as he had rediscovered tonight, that past had not been wasted. He had made his own small contribution to the theatre, then moved on, which was as it should be. But knowing that the theatre was still capable of transforming the realities of its patrons, as this production was doing, made him feel absurdly better about his friends, himself, the craft in general, and the violent events of the last week in particular. In a world that embraced only *Macbeth*, Keyes was not sure that he could exist; certainly he could not thrive. However, in any existence which could contain both the Scottish Play and *The Tempest*, all things were possible. Even happiness, and perhaps love.

So engrossed had he been in the play, he had forgotten for the most part to watch the audience, this having become one of his chief sources of amusement and instruction. He made the time to do this during the second act.

He found no face especially interesting until he scanned the less expensive section of the house. There, surrounded by empty seats, was Kiri Ellison. She was dressed conservatively, for her, in a plain dress that actually concealed much more of her skin than it exposed, and her hair was pulled back in a knot that was almost severe. The beauty thus revealed was magical in itself. Keyes glanced at her several times during the course of the play; she leaned forward, chin in hands, brows knit in concentration, her eyes widening from time to time in appreciation or understanding, especially during Miranda's speeches.

He made a point of looking her way when the last couplet of the play was uttered:

As you from crimes would pardon'd be,
Let your indulgence set me free.

He saw her lean back in her chair for a moment, frowning. Then, her face cleared, her brows relaxed, and she, too was smiling.

Keyes looked for her outside afterwards, but she had disappeared.

(5:2) The river

He knew that there was to be a closing party at The Bells that night, but Keyes was in no hurry to get there, and so took the long stroll to town, via the river. The temperature had dropped, a hint of the winter waiting in weather's Green Room, but it was a bracing crispness, clear and healthy. Near the spot where the bystander swan had met its fate, one of its brothers or sisters sailed sedately along, a rare black swan. Lamplight reflected from an eye, causing the bird to seem to wink at Keyes, who winked back.

Further along, at a poorly lit stretch behind a small bandshell, Keyes stopped to survey the sky. The chill clarity of the night seemed to have brought out an inordinate amount of hard, bright stars. Not only that, but he soon noticed something else which the coming change in season had summoned: a dim series of green-blue lines appeared among the constellations, wavering rays of streaming light that formed a vaguely flower-like pattern. Then, the flirtatious *aurora borealis* began to fade away again, after having appeared to Keyes for only a minute or two.

"Nice night," Keyes whispered to no one at all.

(5:3) The Jester's Bells

When he finally arrived at The Bells, it was to find it packed with people in costume. Keyes had forgotten about this aspect of the closing celebration, so wrapped up had he been in the triumphant *Tempest.* Until recently the end of the Festival season had coincided with Hallowe'en, and when the season was extended to mid-November, the tradition of masquing at the wrap party had moved along with the date. A six-foot penis walked by Keyes, nodding its glans at him as it did so. The walking penis was being chased by Anne of Green Gables and a mummy.

Keyes found a place at the bar and ordered a beer.

"No drinks unless you're in costume," Bruno commanded. Suitably enough, Bruno was attired as Bacchus.

"But I don't have one," Keyes said. "I forgot..."

"No problem," said Bruno, reaching under the bar. He produced a round, red nose of soft rubber, which he affixed to Keyes' face, quickly and efficiently. Bruno continued drawing beer with his free hand, then slid the drink across the bar.

"It's good on you, Claude," Bruno said. "Very good. Looks as if it was made for you, or you for it."

Keyes glanced at himself in the mirror behind the bar. He had to admit that Bruno was right. The red nose perched quite naturally on the lesser nose beneath and looked at home.

"Ever do any clowning?" Bruno asked. He was drawing more beers, but he seemed always able to do that for any number of customers without interrupting his train of thought or conversation.

"Not professionally," Keyes replied, turning his head slightly to get the effect of the nose in the three-quarter view. "Only in my private life, Bruno."

"I don't want to hear about it," the bartender said, moving away.

Keyes took out his pack of cigarettes, which slipped from his hands to the floor. He bent to retrieve them. Suddenly a pair of cloven hooves appeared in his field of vision. As he straightened, he beheld the extravagantly hairy legs of some biped beast, and then an equally hirsute torso, bare beneath the coat which was being flung aside. O'Reilly's outfit was completed by a pair of horns glued to his forehead.

"I see Great Pan is alive," Keyes said.

"Lock up your wenches and livestock!" the actor bellowed as he reached out and tweaked Keyes' rubber proboscis. "Well met, all! Jon-Clod, I see you've found your true calling at last!"

Keyes laughed. O'Reilly was high as the proverbial kite and hadn't yet had a thing to drink.

"Publican! A jug o' punch!"

Bruno understood this to mean O'Reilly wanted his usual. He set up a shot of Bushmill's and drew a pint of Guinness to go beside it.

"There you go, Seamus," Bruno said. "It went well, then?"

There was no answer until the whiskey and a long draft of beer had disappeared down the Irishman's gullet.

"There were many bravos, Bruno— bravos and bravos and arcibravos."

"Congratulations," Bruno said. "I wish I could have been there. That one's on the house."

"Grammercy, noble sir..."

Keyes was so entertained by O'Reilly that he missed Sandra's entrance. When he did see her, she was established at the great man's elbow but was playing her presence down in deference to his success that evening as Prospero. It was unlikely that O'Reilly would play the role again, age and politics being what they were. Like all good actors, Sandra knew when not to call attention to herself. It must have taken every ounce of her talent and skill, dressed as she was.

Sandra had chosen to come to the party as Othello, in blackface and outrageous drag. Her costume was gold brocade above and lavender tights below. Her hair was hidden by a jewel-studded turban. She wore an elaborate earring, and only one. She was carrying a rapier on harnesses at her waist and sporting a superb codpiece.

Beside Sandra, in a pale and nearly transparent nightdress, was someone playing Desdemona to Sandra's Moor, someone who had to be Grace, although Keyes did not recognize her at first. She was wearing a blonde wig and was made up exquisitely. Her meagre lips were fuller; her colour was higher, richer. Her large dark eyes had been made to seem larger and darker. Most remarkable of all was her figure, which Keyes had never before noticed because of the tackiness of her daily dress. Now, in the soft, flowing gown of Desdemona's death scene, Grace's body was revealed.

"Is that Grace?" Bruno whispered across the bar to Keyes.

"I think it has to be."

"She's a stunner."

Keyes nodded. "She certainly is. Amazing what a wig can do."

"Sure, Claude... a wig."

Keyes looked again at Sandra. There was nothing in her face tonight to suggest the anxiety and pain that had marked it during their last encounter. If Sandra was feeling any remorse, it didn't show. It didn't show at all.

The magnificent turbaned head turned. Sandra caught Keyes studying her. There was a flash of recognition in her eyes, a blaze of terrible understanding, but the expression on the dark face did not change. Sandra looked hard at Keyes, then looked through him.

He wondered how she would deal with him, now that she was, in a sense, in his debt.

"There are two kinds of friends," O'Reilly had often said, "those who would hide you from the police if you were in a jam, and those who wouldn't."

Both Sandra and Keyes had heard him say it, and both of them had admitted to agreeing with him.

She'll count on that, Keyes thought, but the power has shifted.

"She no longer has it," he muttered to the still untasted beer which the clown-nose had made him eligible to purchase.

"You're not talking about me, I hope," said a woman seated on the stool next to his. He hadn't noticed her before, but now remembered her vaguely from the old days. He couldn't recall her name, only that she worked on costumes—dyeing or sewing or embroidering.

"No, madam, not about you," Keyes said. "I was talking about a woman who only loves her slaves."

When Keyes looked again across the bar, Sandra had turned away to speak to Grace. Keyes saw Sandra again that evening, but only from a distance.

A corner had been cleared in the back of the pub where instruments and amplification equipment had been arranged, and the band was beginning to tune up. There was a nudge at Keyes' elbow, and he turned to find a white rose at his side, or rather, Betty Beardsley in a white rose suit. "I hope those people are going to play something decent!" she said.

"You'd best watch out, Betty," Keyes said. "Someone will be trying to water you!"

She raised a glass of Scotch to her lips. "I'm looking after that myself," she said loftily. "Very attractive nose, Claude."

The musicians began a jazzy city blues number, and Keyes saw that the vocals were done by three women outfitted as Roaring Twenties flappers: Smoke, Mirrors, and the barmaid Julia crooned a Billie Holiday song about losing a man, but did so with such wide grins on their lovely faces that everyone knew whose loss it really was.

Later in the evening, Hobart Porliss took a turn at the microphone, and gave an astonishing rendition of "Somewhere Over the Rainbow."

Although Keyes was exercising a certain amount of moderation, he found it necessary to make a trip to the washroom. He was drinking beer, which always had that effect on him. When he reached the latrines, he found himself standing beside George Brocken.

"Having fun, Claude?" Brocken asked as he buttoned the fly of his tuxedo trousers.

"Yes, George," he said, then, with much more conviction, "yes, I am."

The crowd was dense when Keyes returned to the bar. His place had been taken by three people: someone dressed as a doctor, in a white coat with a stethoscope about his neck, and two Charlie Chaplins.

"Sorry," Keyes said, squeezing in beside them. The Little Tramp closest to him, he discovered not unpleasantly, was a woman.

"Make yourself at home," she said amiably enough.

Keyes waved at Bruno.

"Where have you been?" the bartender said. "We were looking for you."

"Where do think I've been? I need another beer."

"Coming up, but first there's this." Bruno handed a plain brown envelope across the buxom Chaplin to Keyes.

"A summons?"

"Open it, Bozo, and fix your nose. It's crooked."

"Out of joint," Keyes muttered as he adjusted the red rubber knob.

"Open the envelope."

Keyes was suddenly aware of a hush in the big room. He looked around. Everyone was watching him.

"What the hell is it?"

"Will you stop clowning around and open the envelope?" Bruno growled.

Keyes did as he was told. Inside the envelope there was money, most of it in small bills. There was a round of applause from the revellers.

"I don't get it," Keyes said.

"It's the money from the pool," Bruno explained. "You won it."

"The pool?"

"The Death Pool. A hundred and five dollars. We just made the draw."

Keyes handled the money in a gingerly fashion, as if each of the bills was covered with something nasty.

"I did it," said a small voice, an untrained contralto, from the far end of the pub.

Not quite trusting his ears, Keyes looked down the length of the bar. Grace was standing there.

"I drew your name out of the hat," she said.

Jean-Claude Keyes laughed nervously, then more comfortably, then loudly and for a very long time.

From the notebook of Jean-Claude Keyes:

Today is December 9th– my birthday, which, I see by my calendar, I share with John Milton. I celebrated by finishing the next-to-last draft of Seamus O'Reilly's biography, and mailing off a copy to him in Stratford; I can hear him screaming his protests from here...

I also seem to have quit smoking, for now. At least it will keep me from making another New Year's resolution that I'd only break anyway.

The Stratford police department finally revealed in today's paper that Alan Wales died from a stab wound, but other than that they have made no progress toward apprehending the killer. I suspect that Wales' murder will go down in their files as unsolved.

(5:4) Stratford, deep winter

Soon after the closing party, Keyes had returned to Toronto. He spent a lonely Christmas there, and saw the New Year in with nobody to keep him company but the folks in his record collection— blues singers, most of them. Despite his solitude he kept his drinking to a reasonable level; because of it he did a great deal of work.

In the middle of January, however, he found it necessary to board the train for Stratford once again. He had two reasons for making this trip. The first was to get Seamus O'Reilly's emendations to the penultimate draft of his biography. The second was to celebrate the old actor's birthday, which was January 15th— the Ides of January, as O'Reilly insisted on calling it. No one knew just how old O'Reilly was. Keyes knew he was perhaps a decade older than the fifty-eight he claimed to be.

There had been little news from Stratford since November, and Keyes was content to let the macabre events of that gloomy month slip away behind him into what O'Reilly liked to call the "Mists of Time." Keyes had carried away no souvenirs from his visit to the Festival City, nothing to remind him of his stay there— nothing, that is, except the money he had won in the pool.

He hadn't spent the money, hadn't been able to bring himself even to touch it. The brown envelope lay at the bottom of a desk drawer along with lots of other envelopes.

For reasons that he didn't quite understand, or particularly want to understand, he thought several times of giving the money to Kiri Ellison. He even tried to find out her address, so that he could send it to her.

"Maybe she can buy herself a new dress for the next time she goes to the theatre," he told himself in an attempt to rationalize his desire to make gifts to the girl.

He didn't find an address for Kiri. There was no listing for her in the telephone book.

As soon as he got off the train in Statford, the little city's charm began to work on him. Winter did there what it does to all places: it transforms, creates a quieter, slower world. For some Stratford people the winter was coldly magical; for others a period of desperation. Keyes supposed that most of the town's permanent residents welcomed the winter months as a time of respite from the gypsies and the crowds, although without them the Stratford economy suffered.

"What you lose on the roundabout," Keyes murmured as he walked along the empty streets and glanced into the empty shops, "you gain on the backswing."

He had no idea what to expect of his meeting with O'Reilly. Keyes' publisher had liked the biography well enough to make tentative noises about another book. The subject of this future masterpiece was still undecided, but the possibility of it gave Keyes the sense that he might have a source of livelihood for the next year or so, which was a luxury he had not always enjoyed, and certainly not one to sneer at in hard times.

"A tranquil life," he promised himself of his immediate future, as he approached The Jester's Bells, "but not without interest."

(5:5) The Jester's Bells

O'Reilly was late for their meeting, but Bruno and Julia between them provided Keyes with an excellent lunch, and afterward he passed the time with the newspaper. There were no murders reported in it, or other mysterious deaths, for which he was thankful. There were some curious headlines, however, including one about a robbery which announced:

SUSPECT UDDERS NO PLEA

Keyes borrowed the bar's scissors from Bruno and clipped it for his editorial horror file.

"I sometimes wonder, Bruno," he said as he was clipping, "why the English language doesn't rise up in righteous indignation at maltreatment like this. Everyone else who's suffered abuse is finally speaking up."

"Sounds like you're ready for another beer," the implacable bartender said.

Keyes allowed as how that was probably true, and accepted the glass happily when it came. Already his Stratford imbibing patterns had returned.

"Mr. Keyes?" said a small voice at his elbow.

He paused with his glass midway between bar and lip.

"Miss Ellison!" he said, with a degree of enthusiasm that surprised him. "Sit down..."

She removed her coat and sat, with a grace he had not seen in her before, a very practised grace, which somehow made it all the more charming to Keyes. He noticed that she wore her usual tiny skirt, but with a grey leotard beneath, and a large denim shirt knotted at the midriff; it was a man's shirt.

"Mr. O'Reilly told me you'd be in town today..." she said, speaking more shyly than he remembered.

Mr. O'Reilly? he thought. What's that old goat up to?

"... and I wanted to thank you... for the way... for the things you said."

Keyes shrugged. "I thought you needed a friend."

"I did... you were very kind."

Again Keyes thought about addresses and telephone numbers. Before he could say anything, Kiri broke into a very large smile.

"I'm leaving for Montreal today," she said with undisguised joy in her voice. "Mr. O'Reilly arranged for me to have an interview at the Theatre School. I'm not sure they'll take me, but I always thought I was sort of an actress."

Keyes remembered her performance at The Gilded Lily.

"You certainly have stage presence," he said with a smile.

"You're bad, Mr. Keyes," Kiri said as joyfully as before. "What the hell... it's worth a shot!"

Keyes wished her luck, then stood to give her a hug as she went on her way. She turned back at the door, smiled again, and after a discreet little grind, followed by the most modest of bumps, exited into the street, with her coat slung carelessly over one shoulder, as if she were invulnerable to the winter chill.

O'Reilly arrived soon afterward, under full sail, waving like a weapon the manuscript Keyes had sent.

"You really are a clod!" he boomed. "And you call yourself a friend? This is inaccurate, unseemly, and it's going to take me more time than I have to set you straight!"

"Happy birthday, Seamus," Keyes said.

"I'm too old to have birthdays, but *you*... you obviously need a few more years to polish up your so-called skills. Julia! Bruno! Anyone– medicine for two sick men!"

More drink was served and when Seamus had properly attended to his, he gestured toward the door.

"Was that my friend Kiri I saw leaving?" he asked.

"Your *friend* Kiri? What are you up to, Seamus?"

O'Reilly frowned and looked stern. It was the look he often wore when he was playing a priest or a prelate.

"Up to? Up to! You are a vulgar man, Jon-Clod. For God's sake, the girl is half my age."

"A third your age is more like it," Keyes said. "She's half *my* age."

"What's age got to do with it?" O'Reilly fumed. "I behaved every bit the gentleman that I am."

"That's what I'm afraid of."

O'Reilly ignored this comment, and continued, still in a mildly paternalistic and priestly mode.

"She has a certain raw talent, and a good voice... untrained, but with potential. Also, she is honest and earthy, an unspoiled novice of Dionysus–"

"O'Reilly, I like the kid, too, but she wouldn't know Dionysus if he bit her on the ass."

O'Reilly loomed across the table. "Interrupt me again and your head will be up yours! Let me see... a slender-shanked, dimpled shakti, bright maiden..."

Keyes put his face in his hands.

O'Reilly looked at him. "Not a maiden?"

"I sincerely doubt it."

"All right, then." O'Reilly raised his glass. "Be that as it may, I sent her off to Montreal. I hope she does well."

Keyes nodded his agreement. "So, other than you playing Svengali to Miss Ellison's Trilby, what's been up?"

"You don't know? Didn't I write you? I was going to... ah, well, no matter. I've been given Titus Andronicus and a couple of other very good parts next year."

"That's wonderful news," Keyes said. "You'll make a great Titus."

"To make matters better," the beaming O'Reilly continued, "Sandra and I have been asked to do our Byron routine. Might even get a tour out of it!"

Keyes hesitated, then said. "How is Sandra?"

O'Reilly shook his leonine head in a somewhat bemused fashion.

"She's well," he said, "but strange. She spends most of her time with that little dresser. I don't mean to suggest... I mean, I don't like to speculate on what they're up to."

"They're friends," Keyes said.

"She does seem happier than she has for some time..."

"Good. That's what matters, isn't it? Maybe all that matters."

O'Reilly made a strangely sub-aquatic sound, a sound he often made when he wanted to change the subject. Keyes thought of it as the sound of the Kraken awakening.

"Now," O'Reilly said, making a sweeping motion with his hand across the manuscript, the corner of which was quietly soaking up a small puddle of spilled beer, "as to this sketch of yours..."

"My 'sketch,' as you call it, is nearly finished," Keyes said. "This is the final draft– I'm sending it to my publisher as soon as you've looked it over."

"Finished? Final draft? But you've left so much out!"

"Because I thought it *should* be left out; I don't want to get sued, and I don't want *you* to get sued, either."

"But, Dorabella..."

"I checked with Dorabella," Keyes said. "She's happily married, with three children. Her husband is a C.P.A. in Oyster Bay, New York, and he has no idea Dorabella was in the theatre before she moved to the States; she hopes that he will never find out she was an actress."

"Hmm. 'Actress' is putting it a bit fancifully..."

"Forget about Dorabella. This book is supposed to be an account of your life *on* the stage, not *under* it."

"There's no mention of the *Othello* tour, either," O'Reilly said peevishly.

"The *Othello* disaster, you mean. I still don't understand whatever made you think a one-man *Othello* was a good idea... or why I went along with it."

"It worked," O'Reilly said with grave conviction. "You know perfectly well that it was good... even *you* were good."

"As voices offstage? As all those senators, and as Iago, Cassio, Brabantio, Lodovico... are you kidding?"

"You could never grasp that the action was taking place in Othello's mind– "

"There was no action," Keyes said. "There was only you in gold brocade, declaiming!"

"It worked," O'Reilly insisted. "It felt good; it would have been great, if you hadn't lost my earring."

"Me?" Keyes exclaimed, and once again, for perhaps the hundredth time, they launched into an argument about who had lost the earring, without which (so O'Reilly contended) the character of Othello could not be perfectly portrayed. The argument ended where it always did.

"At least you must admit that the San Francisco performance was a triumph," O'Reilly said.

Keyes laughed. "Yes, It was. What was the name of that theatre? I can never remember."

"The Golden Hind," O'Reilly supplied, beaming. "We brought the house down."

"O'Reilly, the *fire* brought the house down. I didn't think we were going to get out of there... all that smoke. Thank God the audience was small..."

"I had them in the palm of my hand."

"You almost got us killed, you crazy old fool," Keyes said.

"I had to finish the scene, didn't I?"

"You did not have to finish the scene! No one could hear you, anyway... people screaming, bells ringing, sirens..."

"But we were so close to the end." O'Reilly paused, then his chest swelled as he prepared to soliloquize:

Like the base Indian, threw a pearl away,
Richer than all his tribe...

Keyes slowly lowered his head to the table top and rested it on his folded arms.

...Drops tears as fast as the Arabian trees
Their med'cinable gum...

"Ha! I love 'med'cinable gum.' I couldn't stop until we got to 'med'cinable gum.'"

Keyes peeked up at him. "And you didn't stop even then."

"I had to finish," O'Reilly insisted in a voice he might have used if charging the guns at Balaklava. He gestured broadly, magnificently.

...took by th' throat the circumcized dog
And smote him, thus.

The last word rumbled volcanically through the pub.

"You almost got us killed," Keyes repeated.

"Almost, but not quite. We're here, aren't we? What are you complaining about?"

"I know, I know... I shouldn't grumble."

"No, you shouldn't," O'Reilly said. "It was a memorable tour."

"It certainly was that," Keyes agreed at last. "In any event, we started with good material." He raised his glass. "To Shakespeare."

"To Shakespeare," O'Reilly solemnly intoned.

Keyes smiled. This toasting game they had often played before, but usually late at night and never when they were sober.

"Are we drunk?" Keyes asked.

"We are inspired," O'Reilly said, his voice heading toward the upper ranges of his register. "To art!"

"And to justice!"

O'Reilly lowered his glass. "What's justice got to do with anything?"

"Exactly!" Keyes said, knocking back his drink.

O'Reilly signalled Bruno. "Give me a cup of sack, rogue! And bring one for my whoreson friend!"

"Oh, God," the bartender said to Julia. "They'll start singing in a minute."

They did start singing, and they continued to sing– when they weren't arguing– for the rest of the afternoon, and most of the evening.

No one in Stratford seemed to mind.

(5:6) Stratford, the train station

FIRST WOMAN
Do you have our tickets, love?

SECOND WOMAN
Yes, right here... this is so exciting! I've never been to Venice!

FIRST WOMAN
Oh, it will enchant you. I met the most interesting man there, a centaur almost... half horse–

SECOND WOMAN
Really! Sometimes you say the most awful things...

FIRST WOMAN
I say truthful things.

THIRD WOMAN
Excuse me... I have to make a connection to Montreal. Do you know if the train will be on time?

SECOND WOMAN
I doubt it; it almost never is!

THIRD WOMAN
Oh. Well, thanks.

SECOND WOMAN
Do we know her?

FIRST WOMAN
I don't believe so.

SECOND WOMAN
She looked familiar...

FIRST WOMAN
Darling, *everyone* around here looks familiar after a while... But listen, let me tell you about Venice...